ZiPPEL: THE LiTTLE KEYHOLE GHOST

ZiPPEL: THE LiTTLE KEYHOLE GHOST

Alex Rühle

Illustrated by
Axel Scheffler

Translated by Rachel Ward

ANDERSEN PRESS

Andersen Press Limited
20 Vauxhall Bridge Road, London UK SW1V 2SA
Vijverlaan 48, 3062 HL, Rotterdam, Nederland
www.andersenpress.co.uk

2 4 6 8 10 9 7 5 3 1

First published in English in hardback by Andersen Press Limited
Originally published in German as Zippel, das wirklich wahre Schlossgespenst
in 2018 by dtv Verlagsgesellschaft mbH & Co. KG, Munich

The translation of this work was supported by a grant from the Goethe-Institut

British Library Cataloguing in Publication Data available.

ISBN 978 1 78344 844 9

Printed and bound in China by 1010

For Nica and Sophie

CHAPTER ONE

Paul was what used to be called a latch-key kid. Do you know what that is? It's a child who has their own front-door key even if they're quite young. Their parents work long hours so there's nobody there when they come home from school or after-school club. They have to unlock the door themselves. Paul was a child like that.

On the first day of term after the summer holidays, Paul was on his way home from school. He clattered his key along the bannisters as he went upstairs to his flat: *Clong-clong-cling. Clong-clong-clang.*

On the first floor, he met old Mrs Wilhelm, who had her flowery shopping bag with her. Mrs Wilhelm was rather strange. She could often be seen walking up and down the stairs or standing around outside somebody's door.

Sometimes when Mum or Dad opened the door in the morning, she was right there, as if she'd just been eavesdropping on them or looking through the keyhole.

'Hello, Mrs Wilhelm,' called Paul.

'Hello, Paul,' said Mrs Wilhelm. 'I haven't seen you around for a while.'

As she spoke, she was staring at him with her right eye. Her left eye was screwed up tight, the same as ever. This had made Paul very scared of her when he was younger. By now he was more or less used to her only looking at him with one eye, but it was still a bit creepy when she came right up close to him. He could see all the creases around her squinting eye.

'Yes,' said Paul, 'we only got back from our holiday last night.'

'And? Did you have a good time?' asked Mrs Wilhelm.

'Yes, very nice,' said Paul, 'but it was school again today.'

'Oh, no!' cried Mrs Wilhelm. 'Schooool! Is it bad?'

'Uh-huh,' said Paul, who really didn't like school. Not because of the lessons, or his teacher, Mr Ampermeier, who was actually very nice, but because of Tim and Tom, who picked on him every single day. So he generally ended up standing around alone in the playground. But he didn't want to tell Mrs Wilhelm all that now.

'I've got homework to do,' he exclaimed. 'Bye, Mrs Wilhelm!'

'Bye, Paul!' said Mrs Wilhelm.

Paul ran up another two flights of stairs, *clong-clong-cling, clong-clong-clang*, until he came to the flat with *Fellmann* on the door. That was where he lived. With his mum and dad. They were the Fellmanns.

Paul stuck his key in the lock and was about to turn it, when he heard a very quiet voice: 'Ow! Ow-ow-ow. Zippeldesticks, what's all this?'

Paul listened. Was somebody at home already? But the voice didn't sound the least bit like his parents. More like a child. He looked around. There was nobody on the stairs. He put his ear to the door. Nothing. So he moved the key in the lock again.

'Hey!' cried the voice. 'What's this stick doing in here?'

Paul pulled the key out, put his eye to the lock and looked into the flat. He saw the long, empty hallway. There were two half-unpacked suitcases standing there, and at the end of the hall, the parasol and lilo were leaning against the bookcase. It was all perfectly quiet. But hang on, wait a moment, what was that? Paul jumped. To the left. In the darkness. There was something moving. Something white. In the keyhole! Paul jerked his head back. He stood by the door, dead quiet, held his breath and listened.

He wasn't sure, but he thought he could hear someone breathing . . . in the door.

'Is there anyone there?' he asked.

'No-no,' said the voice. 'There's no one here. Nobody there.'

Paul ought to have been startled, but the voice sounded so small and scared that he wasn't afraid. Well, maybe only a little.

Cautiously, he asked: 'Really? Nobody there?'

'Yes-yes,' said the voice, 'no one at all. Really truly, nobody there.'

'So *nobody's* talking?' said Paul.

'Nobody's doing anything, it's just the wind.'

'The wind can't talk,' said Paul.

'Exactly, nor can I,' said the voice. 'I'm no one, no fear. There's nobody here.'

'Will you come out anyway?' asked Paul.

'No,' said the voice and then, a little more quietly: 'I'm scared.'

'I won't hurt you,' said Paul, 'cross my heart.'

It was as though a lamp went on in the lock. Then, for a moment, Paul thought that the lock was blowing

a little bubble of glowing gum. Because the thing that billowed from the keyhole was slowly getting bigger. At first it looked like a little white pea. But it grew from a pea to a ping-pong ball to the size of an orange, stretched lengthways, and gently eased itself away from the door, and floated over to Paul. Paul held his breath and stared at it in silence. Now the thing was as big as the water bottle he took to school. Or his cuddly tiger. It had big eyes and a mouth, and was gleaming white, and it said: 'Good morning.'

'Oh. Erm. Actually, it's getting late, it's five in the afternoon,' said Paul.

The white thing seemed to ponder. Then it said: 'But I've only just got up. Why's it late for you?'

'Because I get up in the mornings. When the sun comes up. And when it goes down, I go to bed.'

'Aha,' said the strange thing. 'The sun. Aha.' Then it sank slowly to the floor. 'Oh,' it went, 'oh-oh-oh.'

It seemed to have little arms. Or wings. At any rate, it was waggling some stumpy little things about in the air, but they weren't much help and the creature sank down lower and lower until it landed on the floor.

Paul crouched next to it. 'Can I help you?'

'No-no. I'm only just learning to float and fly properly. I'll get there.'

'But . . . What are you doing in our door?' asked Paul, sitting down cross-legged on the floor.

'Well, I live in there. Not in the door. I live in the keyhole.'

'Oh, right, yes,' said Paul. 'Sorry. How long have you lived in the . . . in the keyhole?'

'A little while,' said the white creature.

'Ah,' said Paul. 'Were you born there?'

'I'm not bored in my own lock. *You're* the bore. Everything was just right and very, very cosy in there till you came boring into my home with that stick.'

'Oh, I'm sorry,' said Paul. 'I didn't mean to. But why are you living there?'

'What do you mean, why? Where else should I live? I'm a keyhole ghost!'

The little thing said this with an air of pride. It even strutted and stretched a bit taller. Then it floated onto Paul's knee and said: 'That's where keyhole ghosts live.'

'Don't ghosts normally live in castles?' said Paul.

'*I* don't,' said the ghost. 'I live in keyholes. Really truly.' Then it looked questioningly at Paul. 'What sort of castles?'

'You know, big castles. The ones where kings live, and knights and princesses.'

'Are you a king?' asked the ghost.

'No, of course not, I'm Paul.'

'Oh, a Paul. Is that like a knight?'

'No, silly, that's my name. It's what I'm called. How about you?'

The ghost waved its right hand a bit and said: 'Not at all.'

'Your name's *Notatall?*'

'No. I mean I'm not at all cold. I think it's rather warm in here.'

Paul almost burst out laughing. 'No, not "are you cold", what are you *called*? Do you have a name?'

'Don't know,' said the keyhole ghost. 'Maybe . . . maybe Karaputzonogypolatusomow?'

'That's not a name,' said Paul.

'Why not? It sounds really big and dangerous,' said the ghost, spreading out its little arms as if it was trying to scare Paul. It floated to and fro on Paul's knee with a very serious face and a clenched fist. 'Oh, tremble, one and all! You kings and knights and Pauls and all, hear my name and tremble, here comes Karaputzo . . . Ah . . . what was my name again?'

'I don't know,' said Paul.

'Zippeldesticks,' said the ghost. 'Now I've forgotten my own name.'

'Zippel!' cried Paul.

'What?' said the ghost.

'Zippel,' said Paul, 'your name's Zippel.'

'Really truly? How do you know that?'

'I don't know it. I just think Zippel suits you.'

'Really?' The ghost thought. 'Zippel. Aha. Does it sound big and strong and dangerous?'

'Well,' said Paul, 'I think it sounds like a keyhole ghost. Like a . . . '

. . . A very small keyhole ghost, Paul had been going to say, but then he changed it to '. . . like a ghost in the keyhole of a front door.'

'Good. Very good. A ghost in the keyhole of a front door, that's just what I am. So—' Zippel suddenly stopped. 'Shh. Someone's coming.'

He was right. The light had gone on at the bottom of the stairwell. They could hear footsteps. Then the staircase creaked.

'Oh-oh-oh,' said Zippel. 'It must be a grow-nup.'

'A what?'

'A grow-nup.'

'Do you mean a grown-up?' laughed Paul.

'That's what I said. Aren't you listening?'

'And you're scared of them?'

'Oh yes, oh yes, oh yes. Grow-nups are nasty. All of them. Very nasty. One of them stuck a stick in my keyhole earlier, I tried to stop her, but she pushed and shoved and almost squashed me completely. I heard her say, "It will be tricky for a Paul if a grow-nup can't do it." So you won't give me away, will you?'

'I promise,' said Paul, trying not to laugh.

The little ghost flitted through the air towards the door like a ray of light. Then it seemed as though he was sucked in by the keyhole; Zippel grew smaller and smaller, and after two seconds, he was gone. There was a brief glow in the lock and then everything was dark again.

'Hello, Paul.'

Paul's dad had his suit on, as he always did when he came home from work. He looked tired.

'Oh, hi, Dad,' said Paul, who was still crouching in front of the door. 'Did you finish early today?'

It was still the afternoon. Dad didn't normally get home from work until the evening.

Instead of answering, Dad asked: 'Why are you sitting around on the landing?'

'I . . . er, I forgot my key this morning.'

11

'How many times have I told you?' said Paul's dad, pulling his keys from his pocket. 'Before you head out, always stop and think: Have I got everything? Key? Money and—'

'Yes, yes,' Paul interrupted, jumping up. 'I know. Key, money, school bag. But can I have your key please? I'd like to unlock the door.'

'Oh, right,' said Paul's dad, 'sure.' And he gave him the key.

Paul peered into the keyhole, whispered, 'Watch out,' and pushed the key in very slowly.

'What did you say?' asked Dad.

'Nothing, nothing,' said Paul. Then he whispered again: 'I need to turn it now, mind out.'

'Are you OK?' asked Dad, surprised at Paul muttering into the door.

'Yes, yes,' said Paul. 'Fine. How about you?'

He turned the key very carefully.

'Well,' said Dad, 'I'm not too bad.'

As the key turned in the lock, it wobbled a little.

'Oh,' whispered Paul, 'did I hurt you?'

'Are you talking to me?' asked Dad.

'Yes,' said Paul. 'How was work?'

'Work,' repeated Dad. 'Yes . . . well . . .' Dad seemed to hesitate. Then he said: 'Oh, just the same as ever. A bit boring.'

'Oh,' said Paul, not really listening. He'd turned the key right round now. The door opened.

'How was your day?' asked Dad.

'Oh, quite boring too,' Paul lied.

An hour later, over dinner, Paul's mum gave him a terrible shock.

They were eating pasta. Or, to be perfectly honest, eating a pile of mush. Mum's mind had been on other things while she'd been cooking: on her performance next week. Paul's mum was a singer in the opera house. She sang in the chorus. But sometimes she was chosen to sing as a soloist. (Soloists are people who sing all on their own, so everyone can hear any mistakes they may make.) Paul's mum was absolutely mad about singing, but she also got madly nervous if she had to sing by herself. So she was spending the whole time thinking about this upcoming performance and not about the pasta, and now they had to eat rather sticky, mushy spaghetti.

Paul still said that it was delicious, though. Dad said nothing, just ate his pasta in silence.

And then came the thing that gave Paul such a terrible shock. Mum asked Dad if he'd be able to get home from work a bit early on Friday.

'Er, what?' asked Dad, as if he hadn't been listening, 'Why?'

'I told you on the phone today,' said Mum. 'The lock's being changed.'

'Whaaaat?' asked Paul, dropping his fork with the claggy spaghetti. 'Which lock?'

'Uh, the one on the front door,' said Mum. 'We've been meaning to get it sorted out for ages.'

Paul yelled: 'But I love that lock!'

'Since when have you loved our door lock?!' asked Mum.

'It's my favourite lock,' cried Paul. 'Honest. There's no other lock like it. It's got such a great hole for looking through. And . . . and it sounds so lovely when you turn the key. And it smells nice.'

Mum and Dad looked at each other in astonishment.

Then Dad said: 'It's practically an antique. And it's technically very old-fashioned. Nowadays you can get security locks that—'

15

'But you normally love antiques, you love anything to do with history,' Paul interrupted. 'The brown chairs in the sitting room – you always say I have to be careful, they're special because they're antiques. And Mum's opera music is really old and you always say it's the most beautiful music of all.'

'Yes,' said Mum, 'but it doesn't matter whether a lock sounds nice if it doesn't work. And our lock's been sticking for a while when you turn the key. We've been wanting to change it for ages, and it was so bad this morning that I could hardly lock the door, so I went over to see Mr Nitzsche just now, and we're finally getting a new one.'

Mr Nitzsche was the caretaker, who always repaired everything.

'Oh,' said Paul. 'Aha. When will that be?'

'I just told you. On Friday. In three days.'

'Oh, really? On Friday?' asked Paul.

'Hmph, nobody listens to me around here!' Mum exclaimed in annoyance. 'Yes, this Friday!'

Paul looked at his plate of mushy spaghetti and the puddle of ketchup beside it and said nothing more.

The three of them ate in silence for a while, till Mum said: 'Oh, Paul – Dad and I just have to pop out to a tenants' committee meeting.'

'Oh, bother,' said Paul's dad. 'Is that tonight?'

'Yes! I told you that twice as well. What's wrong with you today?'

'Nothing, nothing,' said Paul's dad, attempting to sound light and unconcerned. It sounded pretty odd though. Something definitely wasn't right with him, but Paul didn't really consider it because he was thinking about Zippel, and Mum was cross because nobody was listening to her.

When she asked if Paul would mind them leaving him, he said: 'Oh, sure, no problem.'

'Are you sure?'

'Yes, honest,' said Paul. 'I can even put myself to bed.'

Mum had a moment's surprise, because she normally had to make Paul go to bed every evening, but she sighed with relief. 'Thank you, Paul. We'll be quick. You definitely won't have to go to bed by yourself.'

CHAPTER TWO

His parents had barely left the flat when Paul ran to the door.

'Hey, Zippel, can you hear me?'

'Yes, Zippel can hear, he's got good ears,' sang a voice from the lock.

'Come out a minute, I need to tell you something.'

The ghost just kept singing. 'Paul is there outside, but Zippel wants to hide.'

'Please,' said Paul nervously, 'it's really important.'

'Hey, Paul, don't worry, Zippel can hurry.' And plop, he popped out of the lock.

'What's the matter?' he asked.

'My parents want to change your lock.'

'Whaaat?' asked Zippel. 'Change it? How? When? Why?'

'They say the lock's ancient.'

'Zippeldesticks!' Zippel began floating restlessly to and fro. 'It's . . . it's not ancient at all, it's just the right age. That's not fair, it's my home!' He seemed to have an idea. 'I'll put a spell on your parents.'

'Can you do magic, then?'

Zippel stopped in the air and thought. 'No. But I'll learn. Have you got a book of spells? Get me a book of spells, quick!'

'Um,' said Paul, 'I don't think you'll have time. The locksmith's coming very soon.'

'The lock's myth? Are there stories about your lock?'

'No, the *locksmith*. That's the man who's going to change the lock. It's our caretaker, actually, but he's got a little workshop with tools in the cellar and does all kinds of jobs like that.'

'Oh,' cried Zippel. 'A caretaker. They're bad if they change locks. The baddest grow-nups in the whole world. I'll put a spell on him too! On him most of all!'

Zippel floated to and fro on the landing, waving his little arms around in the air. 'Hocus pocus, fiddle-de-dee, I'll turn the locksmith into a flea!'

He was really very worked up and was glowing whiter than ever in the stairwell. 'No, wait, wait, I know something much, much worse: if he comes the day after tomorrow, I'll borrow his tools. When is he coming, this silly man?'

'In three days.'

All at once, Zippel dropped his arms and sank slowly to the floor like a balloon with the air gradually leaking out. Then he rubbed his eyes and cried bitterly, 'Boo-hoo-hoo-hooo. A keyhole ghost with no keyhole, it's all wrooong. Where will I liiiiiiive?'

'Yikes,' said Paul, 'where's all that dust coming from?'

You see, Zippel was suddenly wrapped from top to toe and back again in threads of dust.

'Oh,' he said, 'exscrews me, I was crying.'

Zippel wiped away the silvery threads, a bit like cobwebs, which trickled quietly to the floor as dust. He wasn't shining nearly as brightly as before, and now he looked more grey than white. Paul swept together the thin threads all around Zippel and picked them up.

'Look at that,' cried Zippel, pointing at the little heap of dusty tears in Paul's hand. 'Caaaan you seeee thaaaat?!'

He now sounded more angry than sad. 'Keyhole ghosts hardly ever cry. Actually never. Sometimes at most. Rarely. But not often. Now and then, you know, but it's very extremely rare.'

'Ah, yes,' said Paul, 'that really isn't often. But it's not as bad as all that. We've got three days to find a new lock for you.'

'It is as bad as all that!' cried Zippel. 'Good grief, that's bad! It's got to be an old lock, you know. With a keyhole that I fit into. A bit oily and a bit rusty and a bit dirty. You don't know anything. Really truly.'

'Oh, OK,' said Paul. 'So what will happen if you haven't got a keyhole?'

'First I'll go grey and then get sick and then – boo-hoo-hoooo!'

The threads of dust started flying around again. And Zippel looked so grey that he reminded Paul more of a flying feather duster than a little, glowing keyhole ghost.

'OK, OK,' cried Paul, 'we'll look for a new old lock for you with lots of oil and rust and dirt. I'm sure we'll find something suitable,' he added, although he hadn't the least idea how to get started. 'But come with me for now.'

Paul went down the hallway to his room. Zippel floated beside him, looking curiously around the hall. Behind him, a last thread of dusty tears fell silently to the floor.

'So this is where you live?' he asked.

'Yes, this is our flat. I live here with Mum and Dad.'

'Wow-ow-ow,' said Zippel, sounding very impressed. 'Your flat is much bigger than my keyhole. Is your dad a king?'

'Oh no, he's a kind of teacher, called a trainer.'

'Really? Like a shoe? So is he hollow like me?'

'Are you hollow inside?' asked Paul in amazement.

'Zigackly. Ghosts are made of air and light and time and nothing else at all. Why are you laughing?'

'Because that's what Obelix says.'

'Is he a ghost made of air and light?'

'Oh no,' said Paul, 'he's a comic-book character. He's best friends with Asterix, and he's made of fat and meat and he's pretty much the opposite of you. But he often says "zigackly".'

'Oh right, oh yes,' said Zippel, who wasn't listening properly now, because by then they'd reached Paul's room. Zippel stopped in amazement in the air and

asked in a whisper: 'Oh, oh, oh, what's this thing here?' He'd spotted Paul's train track, standing in the middle of the room.

'That's my train set,' said Paul, pushing the carriages along the track.

'Oooh!' whooped Zippel, who was glowing white again and bouncing up and down like a rubber ball in excitement. 'Ooh-hoo-hoo! That's amazing! Can I ride in it?'

'Yes, sure, of course,' said Paul.

Zippel floated to the last carriage, shrank to half his normal size and sank gently down onto the roof. Paul was amazed at the way Zippel could just change his size. He'd seen it twice before, when he'd come out of the lock, or vanished into it, but right in the middle of the room it was even more impressive.

Paul pushed the train off and Zippel let himself ride round in a circle.

'Can't it go any faster?' he asked after the first lap.

'Sure,' said Paul and pushed harder.

'Here comes the ghost train,' cried Zippel.

Paul had to laugh. 'Do you know what a ghost train is?'

'Uh, this, here,' cried Zippel. 'That's a train, I'm a ghost, so it's a ghost train.'

'Yes, but there are really big ghost trains too.'

'Oh,' said Zippel, looking excitedly round the room. 'Where are they?'

'Not here, they're much too big for my room. They have them at funfairs. They're so big even grown-ups can go on them. And get scared.'

'What are the grow-nups scared of? They scare *me*!'

'Well, of the ghosts.'

Zippel laughed and laughed: 'They don't need to be scared. I won't hurt them. Really truly.' He shook his head. 'Grow-nups are really daft sometimes.'

'The ghosts on a ghost train are very ugly,' said Paul. 'Gigantic, with blood round their mouths and their eyes hanging out and an axe in their heads, and they groan or suddenly scream.'

'Oh, are they all hurt?' asked Zippel. 'Is the ghost train a hospital for ghosts?'

'No, they're not real ghosts at all, just gruesome-looking puppets to give people a fright. We can go and see when it's Oktoberfest again.'

'Ooh, yes. Tomorrow?'

'No, Oktoberfest is in a few weeks.'

'Afeweeks?' asked Zippel. 'Is that a big city?'

'It's not a place. A week is seven days. Oktoberfest starts in two weeks, so you'll have to wait a while.'

'Oh, right,' said Zippel. 'I'll wait then. What shall we do in the meantime?' He looked expectantly around the room and suddenly shouted: 'Oh, stop-stop! Stop please.'

Paul caught hold of the train. Zippel floated away from the carriage, growing as he went.

'That's awesome,' said Paul, 'the way you can make yourself bigger and smaller.'

'Yes-yes,' said Zippel, not really listening. 'But what's this?'

'My toy shop,' said Paul. He'd had the little shop since he was very young. You could buy mini versions of all the things you get in a supermarket: fruit, milk, bread, washing powder.

Zippel floated behind the counter where there was a metal till. 'No, I mean this here.'

'That's the till for the shop.'

'Ah, and what do you do with it?'

'You put the money in,' explained Paul and opened the little drawer full of one, two and ten cent coins.

'Oooooooooh!' whooped Zippel, floating to and fro again. 'Oo-hoo-hoo! You *are* a king!'

'Me? No. Why d'you say that?'

'You've got treasure. A huge, glittering treasure chest.'

'That's the change. If someone buys something from me, they give me money and I give them something back.'

'Oh-oh-oh-oh, it's so glittery! Who buys things here then?'

'Oh, I used to sell things to my friends, you know. Or Mum and Dad.'

'Don't your parents have their own things?'

'Of course, this is just pretend—'

'Shh,' Zippel interrupted him, listening intently. 'Someone's coming.'

Sure enough, the staircase was creaking with heavy footsteps.

Paul looked around his room. Where could he hide Zippel? He heard a key in the flat's door. Zippel shrank in the air to the size of a pea, flitted into the money drawer of the till and whispered: 'Quick, shut it.'

'Yes, good idea.' Paul closed the till.

At that moment, Paul's mum stuck her head round the door.

'Hello, Paul.'

'Hello.' Paul tried to smile.

'Oh, your shop,' said Mum. 'You haven't played with that for ages. Can I buy something?'

'Er, no, the shop's shut for the night, sorry.'

Mum laughed. 'Fair enough. Shall I read you a story?'

'No, that's OK, I'm really tired,' Paul lied.

'Oh,' said Paul's mum, who normally read to him every evening. 'OK.'

Paul quickly changed into his pyjamas and got into bed. 'Good night. Can you shut the door? The light in the hall is so bright.'

'Really?' said Mum. Normally the door had to stay wide open because Paul was so scared of ghosts and monsters. 'Fine, I'll close it. Sleep well, love!'

'You too,' said Paul.

'Me too,' said Zippel. 'I'm a lovely love.'

Paul's mum had almost shut the door, but she popped her head back round. 'What did you say?'

'Love you,' said Paul. 'Good night!'

'Good night, Paul.'

It was completely dark in the room now. Paul waited till he could hear the TV in the sitting room. Then he jumped out of bed and quietly opened the till again. 'Phew,' he said. 'That was close.'

'Yes,' said Zippel, enthusiastically. 'Very close, merry close, Mummy almost caught a ghost.'

'But where will you stay tonight?' asked Paul.

'I'll go into my keyhole.'

29

'I'm afraid it'll be a squeeze for you. My dad always sticks his key in the lock at night.'

'What? In my lock?' asked Zippel, outraged.

'He doesn't know that it's yours now. He always does that. He says that way he knows where his key is in the morning. But I think it's also to stop burglars getting in.'

'But why should he worry about burgers getting in?'

At first Paul didn't understand what Zippel meant. Then he laughed and said: 'Not burgers, burglars! Thieves. People breaking into the flat overnight and stealing stuff.'

'Let them come – I'd show them!' said Zippel, flailing around with his little arms. 'Come on, come on, come on. I've got to sleep in my keyhole. Can't you pull your dad's stupid key out?'

Paul thought. 'OK, I'll try.' Quietly, he opened his door and looked into the empty hall. He could hear voices in the sitting room. 'Quickly, come on,' Paul whispered, 'they're watching TV.' He ran on tiptoes to the front door.

Zippel overtook him, singing away to himself:

Your parents are watching TV,
Which means they can't hear you and me.

'Shh,' said Paul as he cautiously pulled out the key and set it down on the sideboard. 'OK, in you get.'

'Thank you,' said Zippel, as he floated towards his keyhole. He grew smaller and smaller till he was nothing but a glowing dot. Then even that vanished.

'Sleep well,' whispered Paul.

As he crept back to his bedroom, he could hear Zippel singing:

Sleepy Zippel says goodnight,
Today's been fun and now sleep tight.

CHAPTER THREE

When Paul woke up the next morning, he wondered whether he'd dreamt the whole Zippel business, but then he saw the toy till open, and the train still standing exactly where he'd left it yesterday. He jumped out of bed and got dressed as fast as possible. In the kitchen, he could hear his mother making breakfast. But when he reached the hallway, he got a shock: the key was back in the lock again. Last night, Dad must have noticed that Paul had taken the key out, and he'd stuck it back in again.

Paul ran to the door and whispered: 'Zippel?'

Nothing.

He put his ear to the lock and whispered: 'Hey, Zippel, can you hear me?' Still no sound.

'Morning, Paul.' Mum was standing in the kitchen

door, looking down the hallway. 'Everything OK?'

'Oh, hi, Mum,' said Paul. 'Yes, I just thought I heard a funny noise outside on the stairs. But I must have imagined it.'

'Maybe it was dear Mrs Wilhelm?' Mum said quietly. 'Are you coming for breakfast? It's getting pretty late.'

'Yes, sure,' said Paul. 'I'll just wash my face.'

He went into the bathroom, turned the tap on full so that it sounded like he was washing, and then ran back to the front door. He tapped the wood quietly with his finger, just next to the lock. 'Zippel? Are you there? Zippel! Say something!'

Paul waited a moment, but nothing happened. Then he looked into the lock. It was all dark. Paul's heart lurched. Zippel couldn't have just gone.

Mum called from the kitchen: 'Paul, are you coming? It's nearly half past seven!'

'I'm coming, I'm coming,' mumbled Paul. He hastily turned off the bathroom tap, and went into the kitchen for breakfast with his mum. He was just scraping the burnt bits off his toast when she asked him if there was anything bothering him: 'You're so quiet this morning.'

'Oh, er, no,' said Paul, 'I just don't really want to go to school.'

'I can understand that,' said Mum. 'It's like my performance next week – I'm already so nervous because—'

'Will you make me a sandwich?' Paul interrupted her.

'Yes, of course,' said Mum.

'Great, thanks,' said Paul. 'Can you put something in it this time? Yesterday you gave me two slices of dry bread.'

'Oh, really?' asked Paul's mum. 'I'm sorry, I'm so scatty just now. I've got such a hard role in this opera . . . '

But Paul wasn't even listening. He'd run back to his room, where he scribbled a little note and put it in the shop:

Dear Zippel, where are you? Sorry about Dad's key. I've got to go to school, but I'll be back this afternoon. Hope you will be too. Love, Paul

Then Paul went to school. Which was the same as ever. Tim and Tom picked on him at break time. They picked

on him at lunch. And they picked on him in between, whenever Mr Ampermeier wasn't paying attention. Tim was head-and-shoulders taller than Paul; Tom was twice as broad as Paul. And Paul had no chance against the two of them. At first, he used to hit back when they walked past him in the playground and whacked him or pinched him so quickly that none of the teachers saw. Or he'd run away. But then they used to run right after him. If he defended himself, they seemed to enjoy hassling him even more than normal. Which was why he'd eventually given up. Now he just let their teasing, their nastiness and their insults wash over him. It was like bad weather. If you see dark clouds on the horizon, you hope that the rain will blow over. When it rains, you just have to get wet, and then you wait until it dries up again. The difference between rain and hassle, though, is this: clothes really do get properly dry again, but your soul doesn't. There are words that are so mean they stay stuck in you like a splinter under your skin. Often Paul could still hear their insults in bed at night: *Paul's got no friends. Paul's lonely. Paul stinks. Paul's a stupid idiot.*

Today was particularly bad. Tim stole Paul's sandwich during break, and in art, Tom tipped some of the water from his brush pot down the back of Paul's neck. But even so, today bothered Paul less than normal. He was only thinking about Zippel, and hoping, hoping that he was still there, and that he'd see him again soon. He was just counting the hours until he was finally allowed to go home

again. Eventually, lunch was over. And when after-school club was finally, *finally* finished, Paul cycled home faster than ever before, and leaped up every second step on the stairs.

By the time he reached the top, he was out of breath. He stopped by the flat's door, waited for his heart to stop pounding and his breathing to calm. Then he listened. But there was nothing to hear. He screwed up his right eye and looked into the keyhole with his left. The suitcases were still standing around in the hall. But in the lock, it was still all dark.

He stood up again and said quietly: 'Zippel?'

Outside in the backyard, he could hear a scrubbing noise from a broom. *Sshsht, sshsht, sshsht.* Otherwise all was quiet.

Paul asked again: 'Zippel? Can you hear me?'

Nothing.

Very cautiously, he stuck his key in the lock and turned it slowly. The door creaked quietly open. Paul pulled the key out. He stood in the empty hallway and called out into the flat: 'Zippel? Are you there?'

When there was still no answer, he went into his room.

There was the train set. Just where he'd left it yesterday. The note he'd written that morning was still beside the till.

Paul let his school bag slip slowly from his shoulder and noticed the way the sadness was flooding through him. Zippel was gone. Dad had driven him away with his key. What a shame!

Paul looked out into the yard where Mr Nitzsche was sweeping up leaves and chatting to old Mrs Wilhelm. Mrs Wilhelm was holding her flowery shopping bag and squinting with her left eye, just the same as ever, and she was laughing about something while Mr Nitzsche carried on sweeping. *Sshsht, sshsht, sshsht.* Paul kept his forehead pressed against the cold window and watched the caretaker for at least five minutes, but he didn't even notice that he was looking out. He was just sad. But then he hesitated. And held his breath. Was that someone singing? A child? Quiet sounds. Very close by. Here in the flat somewhere. Paul went to the hall and listened. The noises were coming from Mum and Dad's bedroom. Paul tiptoed down the hall and peeped cautiously around the corner.

His parents' large wardrobe was open. Several drawers had been pulled out and there were socks and pants lying on the floor. Zippel must be hiding somewhere deep in one of the drawers. Paul could hear him singing and rummaging around. Whoops, there came a red sock flying out of the drawer. Followed by a blue one.

Paul's heart made a little jump for joy. 'What are you doing in there?' he asked.

There was a brief moment of quiet in the cupboard. Then there was movement in the sock mountain and, after a few seconds, Zippel emerged from the middle of it. He had a sock wrapped around him like a blanket.

'There are such lovely things in here,' said Zippel. 'Cloaks, blankets. All sorts of things to slip inside.' He sat his little ghostly bottom down on a pair of socks, swayed to and fro and said: 'And such fluffy-soft things to sit on.'

Then he wafted along to the end of the drawer and looked out over the edge. Several pairs of Dad's pants were lying on the floor. He pointed down. 'Hey, um, could I maybe have one of those lovely flags? Maybe that red one there?'

'They're my dad's pants,' said Paul. 'He has a pair for every day and he'd definitely be surprised if there was suddenly a pair missing. I bet I've got something else we could use as a flag.'

'Ha,' cried Zippel, but he suddenly sounded properly angry. 'Your dad! He's a bad man! He's a really horrible person. A real grow-nup. Yes-siree.'

'Why?' asked Paul.

'Why!' shouted Zippel, as if it ought to be entirely obvious why Paul's dad was the nastiest person in the whole world. 'I'll tell you why. Last night, he blocked up my keyhole with his key. I had no room at all and I was crushed and everything hurts and that's not fair and I didn't get a wink of sleep. Really truly.'

'Oh. I'm sorry. But Dad doesn't know that you live in the lock – he didn't do it on purpose.'

'But he did it and it's my lock and now I don't know where to sleep.'

'We'll find somewhere,' said Paul, starting to pick the pants up off the floor and tidy them back into the drawer. 'Promise. But help me tidy up now.'

'What's "tidy up"?' asked Zippel.

were completely gone.'

'I went to school. I wrote you a note, you know.'

'I *don't* know. I can't read.'

'Oh,' said Paul. 'Really? I didn't know that. Shall I teach you?'

Zippel nodded enthusiastically. 'Ooh, yes!'

'OK, come on.' Paul went into his room, sat down at the desk, drew a big A on a sheet of paper and said: 'That's an A.'

'Well, really truly, that's not an A, that's a house,' the ghost contradicted him very patiently.

'Yes, it does look like a house,' said Paul, 'but we read it as an A.' Paul drew another letter. 'And that's an O.'

'No, it isn't,' said Zippel. 'I'll tell you what that is: it's a circle.'

'Yes, that too,' said Paul. 'As a picture it's a circle, but as a letter it's an O.'

Zippel laughed. 'You're very weird sometimes. OK, fine. House and circle. A and O. What else? Do I know everything now?'

'If only,' said Paul. 'There are lots of letters. 26.'

'26? That's more than a hundred! Really truly. And

they all look different? Nobody can learn all that!'

'Oh yes you can. Look: this is an E. E for Elephant.'

'Oh,' said Zippel, 'for elephant?' He was very excited: 'Yes! That's it! Write *elephant*.'

Paul wrote ELEPHANT.

'Hm,' Zippel sounded disappointed. 'Is that it?'

'Yes, why?'

'There's no trunk; I can't see a trunk at all.'

'I didn't draw an elephant, I only wrote it,' said Paul.

'And written elephants have no trunks at all? And no tusks or big ears?'

Paul looked at the word. 'That's not a real elephant, you know. That's just the letters.'

'And where's the real one?'

'In the zoo.'

'Ooh, then write zoo.'

Paul wrote ZOO.

'Finished?' asked Zippel. When Paul nodded, Zippel looked at the word from all sides. Then he picked up the paper that Paul had written on and said: 'I can't see an elephant.'

'Of course not. I just wrote ZOO.'

'But you said the elephant is in the zoo.'

'Well, the real elephant is in the real zoo. These are only the words here.'

Zippel stroked the word ELEPHANT: 'Don't be sad, unreal elephant, when you grow big, you'll get a trunk too.' Then he said to Paul: 'Hey, that was loads and loads of letters already. And really big ones, elephant-sized. I think that's enough for today.'

'I think so too.'

'But how do you know all that stuff?' asked Zippel.

'Our teacher taught us.'

'Oh, your dad?'

'No. My dad is a kind of teacher, but not at my school.'

'What? There can't be two schools?'

'Oh yes, there are lots of schools.'

'Aha, 26 then.'

'Why 26?'

'Because there are "lots" of letters too. "Lots" means 26. You said so yourself.'

'There are even more schools. My dad's a trainer for grown-ups. In a company. He trains people to do things on computers.'

45

'I don't understand all that. But if your dad's a teacher, why was he here at home this morning?'

'He wasn't,' said Paul. 'He always goes out very early in the mornings and doesn't get back till the evening.'

'Well this morning he did leave before you, but when you and your mum were gone, he came back very quietly.'

'What?' said Paul, and then asked in a whisper: 'Where is he then? He didn't hear us, did he?'

'No, don't worry,' said Zippel. 'Just before you came back from school, he went out again. But he spent the whole morning sitting around in your big room. He was talking quietly to himself and staring into a kind of silver box. There were lots of pictures in it and he was hammering on a lot of black buttons really crazy-fast.'

'Ah, the computer,' said Paul.

'Yeah, thanks, smarty-pants,' said Zippel, sounding as if he'd always known what a computer was. 'Then suddenly he looked up with a start at the thing with two little sticks, jumped up and went out again.'

'Which thing with two little sticks?' asked Paul.

'Oh, the sticks that turn slowly round in circles, and it goes ticker-tock all the time, even at night,' explained Zippel.

Paul laughed. 'Ah, the kitchen clock!'

'Yeah, thanks, smarty-pants,' said Zippel again. 'But your dad was so funny, you know. As if he was doing everything in secret. When he went, he opened and closed the flat's door really quietly. And then I went to play in the cupboard with the fluffy-soft things, and then suddenly you were there.'

Paul listened to Zippel and thought. Then he said: 'And Dad didn't see you?'

'Zigackly,' said Zippel. 'For one thing, he's a grow-nup and they're blind anyway. And for another, I hid really well. Look, like this.'

Zippel floated up to the ceiling. At first, Paul could see him climbing, but when Zippel was hovering right up under the white ceiling, Paul could barely make him out against the paint.

'I hovered directly above him,' said Zippel from somewhere up there. 'I even picked up a few little crumbs from the carpet and threw them at him. In revenge for the key in the lock. But he didn't notice a thing. Not a thing.'

'Hm,' said Paul, not really listening. What on earth was wrong with Dad? Paul had been wondering about

him for days, because he'd been so distracted and so . . . so . . . As if he wasn't really there because he was thinking about something else all the time. And now he was secretly sitting around at home?

'Hey,' called Zippel, 'can't you hear me?' He was now floating right in front of Paul's face again.

'Er . . . what?' asked Paul.

'I asked if I can come with you to school tomorrow.'

'Better not,' said Paul, who didn't want Zippel to see how Tim and Tom teased him. 'First . . . first you need to know all the letters,' he said. 'Otherwise you won't understand what we're doing.'

'I know so many already,' said Zippel, starting to sing:

A. O. E. The elephant drinks tea.
E. A. O. To the zoo we go.
O. E. A. Now it's all OK.

'Another day maybe,' said Paul.

'Anuthaday, anuthaday, when purple pandas come to play,' said Zippel. He sounded pretty offended.

CHAPTER FOUR

So that night, Zippel slept in Paul's blue and green sock-sleeping-bag. Or, to put it another way, he tried to. Paul laid the sock on his shelf, well-hidden behind the books, and said: 'Here, this is your bed.'

Zippel looked really unhappy. 'A keyhole ghost always ought to sleep in his keyhole,' he said.

Paul nodded. 'Yes, I know. But for one thing, Dad'll stick his key in there again, and for another, we have to find you somewhere else anyway because of Mr Nitzsche.'

'Nitzsche, natzsche, nubble, I really am in trouble,' sighed Zippel. 'OK, fine, I'll sleep here. But it's far too soft. I need a hard bed. Can't we put something comfy and hard in there? With cuddly corners and edges?'

Paul looked round his room. He grabbed a handful of

marbles, two wooden blocks and a few Lego bricks, and stuffed them all into the sock. 'Better?'

Zippel vanished into the sock and, humming, rummaged around in there. The sock kept bulging out in all directions. In the end, Zippel appeared again and said: 'No oil and no rust and no dust, but at least it's nice and hard and narrow now.'

At that moment, they heard footsteps out in the corridor.

'Right,' said Mum as she walked into the room, 'you really do need to get into bed now. Oh, were you looking for a book for me to read you?' She joined Paul at the bookcase.

'Er, yes,' said Paul, 'right, this one here.' He hastily pulled out a book at random, pushed it into his mum's hand and dragged her towards the bed. 'I'm really tired.'

Mum sat down on the edge of the bed and said: 'Are you sure?'

'Why,' asked Paul, 'what do you mean?'

'Do you really want me to read you this? *Lexicon of Childhood Diseases*? I must have left it in your bookcase by mistake some time when you were ill. Come on, I'll find you a nice story instead.'

She was about to stand up and head back to the bookshelves but Paul grabbed her hand very tight: 'No-no-no, stay here, read me something about diseases – it's really interesting.'

Mum frowned.

'Please,' said Paul, 'there are some really cool diseases.'

Mum shrugged and said: 'All right then.' She flicked through the book a bit and said: 'Here, this bit's interesting: measles.'

'Oh yes, measles, very interesting,' agreed Paul.

So Mum read some things about measles, what they look like and how you tell them apart from chicken pox and rubella, and how long they itch for, and after three minutes, Paul yawned for the first time, and after five minutes he yawned a bit more conspicuously and Mum said, 'Well, you'd better get some sleep.' She stroked his head and turned the light out.

She'd barely left the room when Paul heard a quiet laugh from the bookcase.

'You people have such lovely bedtime stories,' giggled Zippel.

'Shh,' said Paul through the darkness.

But Zippel kept talking and now he sounded just like Mum when she read him a fairy tale: 'Once upon a time, a looong, looong time ago, there lived a teeny-weeny red spot, and its name was Measle. And it went running around someone's skin and met another spot. "O beautiful spot, what is your name?" "My name is Rubellina," said the other . . .'

'Hey, be quiet,' hissed Paul, 'Mum can hear us.'

'Exscrews me,' said Zippel, giggled again and was then finally quiet.

Paul asked: 'How do you do that?'

'Do what?' asked Zippel.

'Well, make yourself sound exactly like Mum?'

'Make yourself sound exactly like Mum,' said Zippel. But this time it sounded like Paul's own echo bouncing off the bookcase.

'Can we have a little quiet here, please?'

Paul jumped. That was Dad's voice. But the door was shut.

'Was that you too?' asked Paul.

'Was that me?' Paul's voice echoed from behind the books.

'Wow, that's mad!' cried Paul. 'Can you copy any voice?'

'Don't know about *any*,' said Zippel in his own voice. 'I only know you three so far, but I can do them pretty well.' He laughed quietly and then said in Dad's deeper voice: 'But we really need to get some sleep now. Zippeldesticks with bells on.'

CHAPTER FIVE

As soon as he woke up the next morning, Paul leaped over to the bookcase, looked behind the books and got a fright: the sock was still there, but Zippel was gone. Paul stuck his head deeper into the shelf, looked left, looked right, but there was no Zippel. He checked behind the books on the other shelves. Nothing. There was a lot of dust everywhere. And behind one of the books was a red marble. Zippel, however, was nowhere to be seen.

Once dressed, Paul looked around his room. There was his unmade bed. The train set. No Zippel. His heap of clothes on the chair. His desk. His school bag. No Zippel. The windowsill. The curtains. The radiator. No Zippel. The play shop. The till. Ah. The toy till. It was open.

Paul ran over to the shop and saw at once that the

coins were gone. All of them. Hmm? Paul kept on looking round his room, but he didn't notice anything obvious. He could hear a quiet sound, though. It sounded like a purring cat, and a bit like a saucepan lid when the steam hisses out of it: *rrrrrrrr-pheeew*. The noise was coming from his desk. And on his desk was his piggybank. Was it grunting? *Rrrrrrrr-pheeew*. The piggybank looked the same as ever: big eyes, open mouth, and the mouth seemed to be making the sound: *rrrrrrrr-pheeew*.

Paul cautiously knocked on the porcelain with his fingernail and instantly, Zippel shot out of the slit on the pig's back, shouting: 'Help, I'm under attack!'

Paul jumped, and Zippel must have got a shock too. He stopped in mid-air and it was only then that he opened his eyes. 'Oh, ah, where am I?'

'Above my piggy bank,' said Paul. He saw that Zippel was a lot greyer than the evening before. 'Did you make yourself a camp in there with all the coins from the shop?' he asked.

Zippel couldn't help yawning massively but still managed to complain, even in mid-yawn. 'Everything's absolutely awful,' he moaned. 'Your dad's sock was faaaaaaaar too soft.'

'What about the piggy bank?' asked Paul. 'Wasn't that any good either?'

'It's not rusty,' said Zippel. 'And, I'm not a piggybank ghost, if you don't mind – I'm a keyhole ghost. I need a lock with metal and oil and dust and it has to be narrow and dark and old. It has to be like that. And I can't sleep and tomorrow the lock's being changed and then I won't have a home at all.'

'Hmm,' said Paul, thinking frantically. 'Perhaps . . . perhaps I've got an idea.'

'You and your ideas,' said Zippel, who looked really

pretty grey. 'What is it this time?'

'We can look all around the building and see if any of our neighbours have an old keyhole that you could live in.'

'Oh, do other people live here too?'

'Of course,' said Paul. 'There are lots of flats here.'

'But then I won't live with you,' said Zippel.

Paul was stumped but tried to hide it by saying: 'Well then, you'll just have to go and sleep in the other keyhole and the rest of the time you can live here.'

'Boo-hoo-hooo,' cried Zippel and the cobwebs flipped and flapped all around him. 'You don't liiiiiiiike me any more.'

'Hey, course I do, I like you a lot,' whispered Paul, raising his hands to comfort Zippel. 'I think you might be my best friend.'

'Boo-hooooo-hoo,' Zippel was still crying:

No one likes me, not a soooul.

I'm so lonely, so aloooone,

That I weep and wail and groooooooan.

And even in my rhymes I mooooooan.

'Paul?' Mum called from the kitchen where she was making breakfast. 'Are you OK?'

'Yes, yes, fine,' Paul called back.

'Have you hurt yourself?'

'No, I'm just listening to a CD. A ghost story. With rhymes!'

'Oh, that's nice,' called Mum. 'Sounds really realistic. Hurry up, though, breakfast's in two minutes.'

'Yes, I'm nearly ready.' Then he said quietly, while carefully picking up the dusty cobwebs from all around Zippel: 'Now, listen, Zippel, this afternoon we'll look for another keyhole for you, and if you like it, you can sleep there, just to try it out, and if not, you don't have to.'

'OK, then,' said Zippel. 'But hurry up with school, it's terribly boring here without you.'

'I will.' Then he went for breakfast.

CHAPTER SIX

When Paul came home that afternoon, he stood in the hallway to listen. Everything was quiet. Well, almost everything. There was an audible, and already familiar, sound coming from the kitchen. Paul crept down the hall towards the quiet *rrrrrrr-pheeew.*

Zippel was lying in the middle of the kitchen floor. In an enormous heap of flour. He'd piled it into a mountain right in the middle of the room, and made a little hollow at the top, in which he was curled up like a sleeping cat. '*Rrrrrrr-pheeew,*' he went, very quietly, '*rrrrrrr-pheeew,*' and every time he breathed out, he blew a tiny cloud of flour off the peak of his little mountain. It looked a bit like the volcano Paul had seen with Mum and Dad last year in Italy, where little clouds of

steam puffed away from its summit all day long.

Paul walked softly to the sink to get himself a glass of water. He crept really cautiously around Mount Flour, but Zippel must have heard him anyway. He opened his eyes. Then he stretched, in a very similar way to people when we wake up. But when he did it . . . ! First, he stretched his right arm to the right, and it grew longer and longer and longer, almost like a rubber band. Then he stretched his left arm to the left and his right arm shrank again while the left arm extended way beyond the flour mountain. He yawned, elongating his head, which stretched very long and thin and tall. Finally, he shook his whole body like a dog or a cat shaking its wet fur once through from top to bottom. Now he looked just the same as ever, except that he was proudly sitting at the summit of his little mountain.

'Just look at this! Such gorgeous dust! The loveliest I've ever seen.'

'That isn't dust though,' said Paul.

'Oh, yes, it is. It's sleeping dust. Dust that I can finally get a really lovely sleep in.'

Paul shook his head. 'That's flour. You cook with it.'

'Look with it?' Zippel blew out his cheeks.

'Cook,' said Paul. 'Bake cakes. Or bread. Things to eat. And that's why I've got to clear it off the floor. If my parents see a heap of flour on the floor, they'll be cross.'

Paul was just about to get the dustpan from under the sink when Zippel asked: 'What's eating?'

Paul stopped and stared at him in amazement: 'You really don't know what eating is?'

'Don't think so,' said Zippel.

'Wow,' said Paul, and thought for a moment. Then he said: 'Eating's like this,' and he took a roll from the bread bin.

'What's that?' asked Zippel.

'A bread roll,' said Paul. He tore off a piece, held it between two fingers, opened his mouth, popped it in, chewed a few times and swallowed it down.

Zippel watched him, aghast. 'Where . . . where's it gone?' he asked.

'Uh, in my tummy.'

'Open your mouth,' said Zippel agitatedly, 'open your mouth right now.'

Paul sat on one of the kitchen chairs and obediently

opened his mouth. Zippel flew right up to it and looked in curiously.

'Tongue up!'

Paul rolled up his tongue.

Zippel looked in every corner of Paul's mouth.

'Where's the roll?'

'Uh, swallowed down,' said Paul.

'Stand up a minute.' Zippel fidgeted. 'Go on, go on, go on, get up.'

Paul stood up. Zippel looked first at the chair and then at Paul: 'I don't believe it. How do you *do* that? Pull up your jumper.'

Paul pulled up his jumper and his T-shirt. Zippel flew right up to his tummy. He pressed his ear against it and said quietly: 'Hello? Roll? Hello? Are you in there?'

Then he floated right round Paul, once, twice. 'Own up,' he said. 'You've hidden it somewhere. You haven't really thrown it inside yourself at all.'

'Yes, I have,' said Paul.

'Zippeldesticks!' Zippel cried with delight, clapping his hands. 'You can do magic!'

'No, no, I just ate it.'

'Yes, but where did it go then?'

'In my tummy.'

Zippel looked enthusiastically at Paul's tummy and said: 'Can I eat something too? A piece of roll?'

'I think that would be too big for you,' said Paul. 'Wait a bit.'

He pulled a bag of raisins out of the cupboard and held it out to Zippel.

Zippel looked very disappointedly at the raisins. 'What's that brown, wrinkly stuff?'

'They're raisins. They're yummy.' Paul popped three raisins in his mouth, chewed for a while and then swallowed them down.

Zippel took a raisin, opened his mouth really wide, cautiously slipped it in and hastily shut his mouth again.

A gentle plop. The raisin lay on the kitchen floor, directly below Zippel.

'Oh,' said Zippel.

'Oh,' said Paul.

They both looked at the raisin lying next to the flour.

'Maybe I need to keep it in my mouth for longer,' said Zippel.

He took another one, popped it in his mouth – plop. The second raisin was lying next to the first one.

'Hmm,' said Paul, 'they just fall right through you.'

'Pity,' said Zippel.

'Oh well, at least you can't get a tummy ache. But I really have to sweep up the flour now,' said Paul.

'Can you eat the flour too?' asked Zippel.

'Well, that's too dry. But here, look,' Paul opened the fridge. 'You can eat pretty much everything in here.'

Zippel floated into the fridge.

'Oh, it's icy cold in here. What's this hard lump?'

'Butter,' said Paul.

'**Butter's for nutters,**' sang Zippel, still floating there. 'And the red jar?'

'Jam,' said Paul.

'**Jam, wham, bam.** Oh, and this here, these yellow strings?'

'That's a pot of spaghetti. It's pasta. Mum burnt it yesterday evening.'

'They're so pretty,' cried Zippel. 'Like really, really long hair. So golden and brown and black underneath.'

Paul took out the little pot of spaghetti.

Zippel grabbed two strands and wrapped them several times round his neck. Then he floated around the kitchen, holding the spaghetti necklace daintily in his fingers like an elegant lady and sang:

Spaghetti-neckletti, long and smart
Spaghetti-neckletti looks the part.

Suddenly he stopped in mid-air, looked at the spaghetti in the pan and said: 'But you can't eat anything as big and long as that, can you?'

'Of course I can,' said Paul. He took a fork, wound up a few strands of spaghetti from the pan, stuck it in his mouth and gulped.

'But,' said Zippel. 'But, but, but . . . There's no room left in your tummy! Isn't the roll still in there?'

'Oh, you can fit quite a lot in,' said Paul.

'And then it stays in there forever?'

'No, it starts off in my stomach, then it gets digested, and eventually I go to the loo and do a poo.'

'Poo?' asked Zippel eagerly.

'Yes. And wee.' Paul explained to him what they were.

'Wee?!' Zippel sounded even more enthusiastic.

'Poo and wee? Those are really good words. Poo and wee! They sound like two best friends.'

He sang:

Poo-Poo and Wee-Wee were two friendly fellows.
Poo was the brown one and Wee was all yellow.
Wee was a liquid and Poo was rather harder,
And both were what's left of the food from your
　　larder.

'Aah, I understand now,' said Zippel. 'The round thing's called a roll because it rolls through you. And the pasta gets passed through your tummy until it comes out again.'

'Maybe,' said Paul. 'But anyway, I need to clean up the flour now.'

'No problem; I'll help.' Zippel used both hands to lift the glass of water from beside the sink, and then he poured it on the floor.

'Hey, what on earth are you doing?'

'Water's great for washing things away,' said Zippel.

Paul hastily grabbed a handful of tissues and threw them into the huge puddle. The tissues sucked up the water. 'Whoa, Zippel, you can't just pour water around in the flat. You have to sweep the flour up with a broom.'

'Exscrews me,' said Zippel, 'I didn't know that.'

Paul threw away the soggy tissues and swept up the flour. Then he said: 'There. I'll just go to the loo. And then we've really got to go out onto the stairs to look for a keyhole for you.'

'Oh,' said Zippel, 'can I come to the loo too? I want to see it.'

Paul shrugged. 'If you really want to.'

CHAPTER SEVEN

Paul walked to the bathroom with Zippel floating along behind him.

'Hey, look at that,' he said when he saw the toilet bowl, 'a white chair.'

'That's the loo,' said Paul. He lifted the lid.

'Oh,' cried Zippel, anxiously, 'mind out, mind out, mind out.' He ripped the fat toilet roll out of its holder and threw it into the loo. There was a splash, then the whole roll soaked full of water.

'Hey! What are you doing now?' yelled Paul.

'Cleaning,' cried Zippel. 'There was water. Right in the middle of the loo. That's not right! That's not allowed! You said so yourself. Water needs clearing up right away. Really truly.'

'But, Zippel, there's meant to be water in the loo,' said Paul, pulling the dripping wet toilet roll out of the bowl and throwing it in the bin.

'Oh, right,' sighed Zippel. 'Exscrews me. I didn't know that either.'

'*Excuse* me,' said Paul, pulling down his trousers and sitting down to wee.

'Don't mention it,' said Zippel, sounding very generous.

'No, I mean, you always say "exscrews me". But it should be *excuse* me.'

'Well I say *exscrews* me. It sounds much better. You screw up and then you say exscrews me.'

'Have it your own way,' said Paul, as he started to wee.

'Oh, that's such a nice noise,' cried Zippel. 'Listen to it tinkling. Beautiful.'

Paul stood up, pulled up his trousers and pressed the flush.

'Help!' shouted Zippel. 'Watch out! Stop!' He stared at the rushing water. Then he looked at the floor. Then back to the water, rushing through the toilet bowl. And then back to the floor in front of it. 'Fancy that,' he said. 'The floor didn't even get wet.'

'No, it all goes down the drain here,' said Paul.

Zippel was watching the rushing water in fascination.

'So you've got a waterfall right in your flat? That's so . . . so . . . Can I fall some water too?'

'Flush it, you mean?'

'Yes. Please-please-please. I want to flash it.'

'Flush,' Paul corrected him. 'Sure. But you'll have to

wait till the tank's filled up again. And then you press down on this lever here.'

Zippel jiggled up and down by the tank, waiting for the water to refill. He stroked the cistern gently and said: 'Nice water tank, kind water tank, be good and fill up with lots of lovely water, yes?' Then he pressed the flush and yelled: 'Waterfall! Waterfaaall! Look out, look out! A thousand hundred litres, ta-ran-ta-raaaa!'

He floated excitedly over the bowl, flailing his little arms around as if he were conducting the water. Once it had all gurgled away, he looked enthusiastically at Paul and said: 'Again.'

'Go on, then,' said Paul. 'But then we need to go. Mum and Dad will be back at some point.'

'Soon-soon-soon,' said Zippel as the flush roared again. 'Waterfall! Waaaterfall!' Zippel was bobbing up and down faster than ever, laughing and clapping and singing a little flushing and roaring song, but you couldn't hear it over the flushing and roaring water.

Paul went back into the hallway and fetched his key. He waited a while, but after Zippel had flushed a fifth time, he said: 'Come on, that's enough now.'

'OK,' said Zippel, 'fine, but I'll carry on later. Oh boy, that's sooooooo cool. A waterfall! In the middle of the flat. Really truly.'

'Yes, yes,' said Paul, 'but be quiet now and come *on*.'

CHAPTER EIGHT

Paul took his key, opened the flat door a crack and listened for anyone coming. He couldn't hear a thing.

'Come on, then,' he whispered. He peeked quickly over the bannisters to see if he could see anyone. Nothing.

Zippel, who was floating beside him, also looked down the three storeys. 'Hoo-hoo-hoooo!' he yelled excitedly. 'What a lovely long way down. And what's this pipe?'

'Do you mean the handrail?' asked Paul.

'Dunno if I mean the randhail. I mean this wooden slide that goes whee-whee-whee all the way down.'

'Yes, that's the handrail.'

Zippel floated onto it and then slid down one storey at a time into the depths.

He sang:

Oh yes, the shiny hand-and-rail
Goes down and down and round the trail:
Handrail, doornail, tell-tale, derail.

Zippel grew quieter and quieter and smaller and smaller. When he was right downstairs, he called up: 'Come on, your turn!'

Paul shook his head: 'I'm scared.'

Whoosh, Zippel popped right up the middle of the stairwell. 'Why?'

'If I fell, I'd be dead.'

'Oh. Dead? What's dead?' asked Zippel.

'Um, if you're dead, you're not here any more,' said Paul.

'What? Not here any more? Would you be hiding down there, then?' asked Zippel. 'Ooh, go on! Jump down!'

'No, if you're dead, you stop living,' said Paul.

'How can you stop living? You just keep on all the time.'

Paul looked at Zippel in surprise: 'Can't ghosts die at all then?'

Zippel thought for a moment: 'Don't think so. At any rate, I've never died. Have you?'

'No, I haven't. Otherwise I wouldn't be here. But my grandma died two years ago. And Mr Wilhelm died here in the house not long ago. Old Mrs Wilhelm's husband.'

'And where are your grandma and Mr Wilhelm now?'

'In heaven, maybe,' said Paul.

'That's a very long way up,' said Zippel. 'How did they get up there? Can you people fly after all?'

'Their bodies aren't up there,' said Paul, 'they're in the cemetery. But their souls are.'

'What on earth is that?' asked Zippel.

'A soul? I don't really know,' said Paul. 'Really, I've always imagined a soul as a bit like you, something small and shining, all light and white, and it can fly.'

'Oh, how nice! Do people all have a keyhole ghost hidden inside them?' Zippel flew right up to Paul's eyes, looked deep into his pupils and said: 'Little Paul-ghost, will you come out from Paul and see me?'

'My soul can't come out,' said Paul, 'it always stays inside me.'

'You just said it could fly,' said Zippel. 'You people are

really weird. You've got all that food inside you. And now there's a soul too. You must be really full up. Rolls. Flying souls. Pasta. But Paul, where are all the keyholes I can live in?'

'Exactly,' said Paul. 'We need to go round all the doors in the house.'

So they went down to the ground floor – that is, Paul ran down, in which time, Zippel slid right down the whole 'hand-and-rail' six times. Then they ran up one flight of stairs at a time, but all the other flats in the building had very modern locks: all narrow with a tiny slit instead of a proper keyhole to look into.

'I'm not a slit ghost,' moaned Zippel, 'I'm a keyhole ghost. What are they all thinking of?'

'Yeah, it's silly,' said Paul, once they'd reached the sixth floor. He glanced quickly at the last few front doors and was just thinking that that was it when, right at the end of the dark corridor, he saw Mrs Wilhelm's door.

Her door was very different. Much older. And the keyhole was really big, even bigger than the one at Paul's home.

'Ooooh,' said Zippel in delight, 'what a lovely keyhole.'

Even as he spoke, he was shrinking, and then *whoosh*, he was gone.

'Ooh-oo-ooh!' Paul could just hear him from outside. 'Hoo-hoo.' Then he heard Zippel rummaging and rustling around inside the door.

'Zippel?' asked Paul.

It was silent for a moment, and then the little ghost reappeared and grew large. He was shining brighter than normal and sounded really thrilled. 'Oh, Paul, if only you could see that!'

'Why? What's up?'

'That's what I call a *lock*! Just how a lock ought to be. With very ancient springs. And there's lots of space and it smells great. And it's all so nice and rusty and oily. Oh, Paul, I've got to go back in. It's the perfect keyhole-ghost keyhole.'

Before Paul could say a word, Zippel had gone again. This time he stayed away for longer. Paul could hear two pigeons cooing outside in the gutter. But it was very quiet in the keyhole now.

'Zippel?' Paul whispered after a while. 'What are you doing?'

No answer. Had he fallen asleep in there?

'Hey, Zippel, come out, I don't want to stand around here alone.'

Silence. Paul was just about to sit down on the stairs to wait when the door to Mrs Wilhelm's flat popped quietly open.

Zippel appeared in the doorframe. 'Come on in,' he whispered excitedly.

'You can't do that,' Paul hissed. 'What if Mrs Wilhelm sees us?'

'She's not even here,' said Zippel.

'All the same. It's breaking in.'

Zippel zipped around. 'Oh, break it in, break it out, break a leg. I just want to show you something. Really quickly. Hurry up.'

'This really isn't right,' said Paul, hurriedly glancing over the bannister to check if anyone was coming.

'It is so right,' said Zippel. 'I've found something you need to see.' He vanished into the flat again.

Paul felt very uneasy as he pushed the heavy old door open. It squeaked so loudly that he jumped and looked round in case anyone could see him.

A long, empty hall. On the walls were old picture frames. Paul stepped nervously through the door.

'Hello?' he asked cautiously. 'Mrs Wilhelm?'

Silence.

He walked slowly down the hall. The floorboards creaked under his feet. He stirred up dust that danced in the slanting beams of afternoon sunlight.

'Zippel?' asked Paul quietly. 'Where are you?'

'Here,' Zippel yelled enthusiastically from the very far end. 'Ooh-ooooh! In the sitting room. Hurry up. You've got to see this.'

Paul walked on down the hall, past the picture frames. To his surprise, they were all empty. There were no pictures in them. 'Weird,' he said. 'Did you see that, Zippel? The fra—' Then he stopped. Open-mouthed. In the sitting room doorway.

The room was quite large. In the middle were two beautiful old upholstered armchairs. Between them was a small table. Opposite the chairs was a wide bookcase. Really wide. And as high as the ceiling. And on the shelves were nothing but locks. Nothing else. Old door locks. Side by side. Large iron locks. Small ones that looked gilded.

Fat locks, thin locks. But all with big keyholes. Lying next to some of the locks were their keys.

Zippel hovered by the bookcase, whooping quietly. 'Can you see that?' he cried, positively glittering with happiness. 'See that? Canyouseeeeeethat?'

Paul nodded. 'Yes,' he said, quietly, but Zippel had already vanished into a fat, round lock. 'Oo-hoo, what a smell,' he called from inside, 'smells of twenty-two-hundred-year-old oil.'

Then he came out again – and vanished into the next lock, a square one that even had its gilded door handle still attached. Paul sat in one of the two armchairs, which were positioned so as to look straight at the shelves of locks.

'And there's loads of rust in here, glorious,' enthused Zippel from a highly-decorated lock. 'And dust – just right, just exactly right! I really like this Mrs Wilhelm.'

Little clouds of dust and rust flew out of the lock.

Why would someone collect old locks? Paul wondered. Where had Mrs Wilhelm got them all from? And why had she displayed them like valuable paintings and cleaned them like precious treasure?

'What a cheek,' said a sudden voice behind Paul. Paul jumped. Mrs Wilhelm was standing in the half-darkness of the hallway. She had her left eye screwed up more tightly than ever. 'What are you doing in here?'

Paul leaped up. 'Oh, sorry,' he said. 'I . . . Um . . . '

Mrs Wilhelm put her head on one side. There was a deep frown on her brow. She was looking at Paul with her large right eye and waiting for him to carry on.

'Your door,' said Paul. 'Well . . . It was open. I was just going to the attic when I saw the open door and I called out to you and then I accidentally went in and—'

Mrs Wilhelm listened to his stammering. She seemed to be growing angrier – the frown was getting deeper and deeper, and she interrupted him crossly: 'You don't

go into other people's flats. Not even accidentally.'

'Yes, I know, I agree,' said Paul. 'That's what I said. Er, to myself.'

'But you walked in anyway?'

Paul stared at the floor. 'Sorry, Mrs Wilhelm,' he said quietly.

'I thought better of you, Paul,' said Mrs Wilhelm. 'Go home, now, please.'

'Yes,' said Paul and nodded, without looking up, 'I was just about to.'

He walked past Mrs Wilhelm in the hallway, muttered 'Bye' without turning round, and stumbled out to the stairs. He ran down the first flight. Then he waited for Zippel. But Zippel didn't come.

'Bother,' Paul whispered to the empty stairwell. What should he do now? He couldn't exactly ring Mrs Wilhelm's doorbell and ask if his ghost was still there. He waited another minute and then went down to the flat and into his room.

Zippel was already there, sitting on the edge of the play shop.

'There you are!' said Paul and Zippel at the same time.

'I was waiting for you,' said Paul.

'Me too,' said Zippel. 'Well, not for me, but for you.'

Paul sat on his bed.

'That Mrs Wilhelm is super-duper,' gushed Zippel, 'a really good grow-nup at last.'

'Wow,' said Paul. 'She's hopping mad.'

'Yes, but she's got great taste – those were amazing keyholes.'

'Maybe, but I'm scared that she'll ring the doorbell tonight and tell my parents that I was sneaking around in her flat. And then I'll be in trouble with Dad again.'

'I don't think so,' said Zippel.

'What don't you think?'

'That your dad will tell you off.'

'What makes you think that?' asked Paul.

'Well,' said Zippel, 'he's sneaking around in a flat every day himself.'

'What do you mean?'

'Well, this morning. When you and your mum had gone. He came creeping back in here again.'

'What?' shouted Paul. 'Really? Why didn't you tell me earlier?'

'There was so much going on,' said Zippel. 'First the kitchen, then the amazing waterfall in the loo and then Mrs Wilhelm. Anyway, that Mrs Wilhelm, she—'

'And what was Dad doing here?' Paul interrupted the torrent of words.

'Nothing. He sat around for hours, stared into the computer for ages and bashed about on the buttons and eventually he ran out again. I'm not a human, so I might be wrong, but if you ask me, he didn't look very cheerful.'

Paul was completely confused. Who could his dad be hiding from? And why was he acting so oddly? Or was Zippel making it all up?

'Anyway,' Zippel said, 'all I wanted to say was that your dad can't exactly tell you off if Mrs Wilhelm comes. He's sitting around in secret in a flat too.'

'That's different though,' said Paul. 'This is *his* flat.'

CHAPTER NINE

The next morning, Paul cycled to school, just as he did every day. He had to ride down Three Mill Street and then along the stream. He was just looking up into the trees, where two squirrels were playing chase, when he heard a quiet voice singing:

School's not very far away
Zippel's going to learn today.
How to count and read and draw,
And all one hundred numbers, for
Zippel's got a plan to be
The brainiest ghost you'll ever see.

Paul braked suddenly. He stood right in the middle of the cycle path and twisted round to peer at his school bag.

'Oh, no, Zippel.'

'No-no,' said Zippel, 'I'm not here. Not at all. That was just a sort of little song floating about by itself.'

'Of course you're here,' groaned Paul. 'But I told you: I can't take you today.'

'You aren't taking me at all,' said Zippel. 'I just float into your school bag all by myself, and your school bag gets taken to school, and then I just happen to be at school too. You ride on and don't worry about it.'

Paul wondered whether he should take Zippel back home. But then he'd be late.

'OK, I'll bring you,' he decided. 'But school is heaving with grown-ups. What if they see you? You have to be really quiet. Promise?'

'Yes-yes-yes,' said Zippel. 'You have my solemn premise.'

Paul rode on. Zippel was quiet for a while. Then he said: 'Hey, Paul.'

'What's up?' asked Paul, without stopping.

'There's some kind of jar in here next to me. It wobbles to and fro all the time. I'm afraid it'll fall over. Can you take it out?'

That must be the strawberry yoghurt Mum had given him for a snack. 'Yeah,' said Paul. 'I will when we get there.'

Five minutes later, they arrived outside the school and Paul parked his bike. He looked all around to check that

nobody was watching him. Then he quickly put his bag on the ground and opened it.

Zippel was sitting on the books, grinning at him. 'By the time we get home this afternoon, I'll be able to read all that,' he said, rubbing his hands. 'Then you can pick a book and I'll read it to you, OK?'

Paul took out the jar of strawberry yoghurt. At that moment, Tim and Tom came round the corner. 'Oh no,' muttered Paul.

'What's wrong?' asked Zippel. He was about to peek over the edge of the bag.

'Shut up,' hissed Paul, hurriedly closing the bag. He was holding the yoghurt in his hand, which meant it took longer than usual to do up the two straps. Just as he was about to put the bag on, Tim and Tom looked over his shoulder.

'Oh, this looks nice,' said Tim. He took the jar from Paul's hand. 'Strawberry yoghurt! Yum! My favourite. Thanks!' Tim kept hold of the jar and just walked away without looking round.

Paul stood there, empty-handed. Tom laughed. 'Paul's self-service shop. We'll come here for all our morning snacks from now on.' Then he ran off after Tim.

The whole scene had taken just a couple of seconds. Tim had taken Paul's snack as if it was the most ordinary thing in the world. As if it actually belonged to him.

Paul had a salty taste in the back of his throat from biting back the tears that were rising up inside him. Just don't cry now. That was what they were waiting for. He picked up his bag and went on towards the school. Ten metres ahead of him, he could hear Tim and Tom laughing.

And directly behind him, in his school bag, he could hear a small, angry voice. 'Revenge!' huffed the voice. 'That was the very meanest meaniness in all the world! Just wait till I get hold of you two – I'll squish you into a ghostly mush!'

'Shh,' whispered Paul, trotting quietly into the classroom.

Tim and Tom had already hung their jackets over their chairs and were sitting in their places. 'Hey, here's Paul,' cried Tim, as if he were really pleased to see him. 'Good morning. How are you?'

Paul walked in silence past the two of them and sat down in the back row.

CHAPTER TEN

First, they had science. Mr Ampermeier had brought lots of little plastic trees and the children had to tell him their names: birch, fir, spruce, beech . . . Once he asked Paul what type of tree had a white trunk. Paul hadn't been listening because he was still so furious. Because of the stolen yoghurt, obviously, but also because he knew that Zippel had seen Tim and Tom being so nasty to him. His heart was pounding and he was still having to hold back the tears that were welling up behind his eyes like water behind a dam. That made him even more furious. The fact that those two kept making him cry was the nastiest thing of all. So now, when Mr Ampermeier asked him what that tree was called, the one with the white trunk, Paul just shrugged his shoulders. 'Don't know.'

'Come on now,' said Mr Ampermeier. 'You know this. White trunk. Green leaves.'

'I don't care,' said Paul.

Mr Ampermeier frowned: 'Is something wrong?'

Paul almost said: 'Yes, there is! They stole my strawberry yoghurt.' But he just muttered: 'No, no, it's fine.'

Mr Ampermeier gave him another searching look and then shrugged too, saying: 'OK, fine, who can answer my question?'

Lots of hands went up and Tim shouted: 'You must mean a birch, Mr Ampermeier!'

'Yes,' said Mr Ampermeier, 'but don't just shout out, Tim.'

'Sorry, Mr Ampermeier,' said Tim, as if he were an absolute model pupil.

Then they carried on with other trees, and twenty minutes later, Mr Ampermeier said: 'So, now let's all go out into the playground and see what kinds of trees we can find there.'

Most of the children jumped up immediately from their chairs. Paul took his time – he didn't want to speak to anyone. As he walked out, he saw Tim and Tom trying to hide in the classroom. But Mr Ampermeier spotted them too and called out: 'Go on, you two, out you go!' Tim and

Tom shuffled, grumbling, into the corridor.

Outside, they were all standing around while Mr Ampermeier pointed to an evergreen tree on the edge of the playground and asked what it was. Someone said: 'fir'. Mr Ampermeier said: 'correct' and asked about the next tree.

Fifteen minutes later, when they walked back into the school, there was a rather sickly-sweet smell in the classroom. Lotti, who sat two rows in front of Paul, said: 'Smells of chewing gum in here.'

'Nah,' said Johanna next to her, 'more like fruit muesli.'

But Mr Ampermeier said it must be coming from outside and carried on with the lesson.

When the bell went for break time, everyone jumped up. Tim and Tom hastily pulled on their jackets. Tim was just walking through the classroom door when he shoved both hands into his jacket pockets – and froze. His eyes grew bigger and bigger. He was standing in the doorframe with a cluster of other children behind him, who all wanted to get past and were now staring to see why Tim had stopped. He slowly pulled his hands from his pocket. Pink slime dripped from his fingers.

'Eww,' screeched some of the girls behind him.

93

Now Tom, who was standing by the board, also pulled his hands from his pockets. Same thing: big eyes. Astonishment. Pink hands, dripping onto the floor.

'Oh, that's what the smell was,' giggled Selina. 'Strawberry yoghurt.'

Tim and Tom looked at each other. Then they both glared with hatred at Paul. 'Did you do this?' asked Tim.

'N . . . n . . . no,' stammered Paul. 'How could I? When?'

'What's all that yoghurt?' asked Mr Ampermeier.

'It's Paul's,' said Tim and Tom in one voice.

'Oh,' said Mr Ampermeier, 'so how did it get into your jacket pockets?'

'Don't know,' said Tim.

'No idea,' said Tom.

Little pink lakes were forming around the two of them as the yoghurt carried on dripping from their hands. And it was oozing from their jackets too.

'Can you explain this?' asked Mr Ampermeier, looking at Paul as he spoke.

'Um, well,' said Paul with a shrug, 'They took it off me this morning outside school.'

94

'Why did you take Paul's yoghurt?' Mr Ampermeier asked.

'Because . . .' Tim shrugged. 'It tastes nice, I guess.'

Tom said nothing.

'You two, go to the toilets, wash your hands and clean your jackets,' ordered Mr Ampermeier. Then he pointed to the pink puddles on the floor. 'After that, you will wipe up this mess, and we'll talk.'

Paul went out to the playground. Max stood beside him. 'Those two are real idiots,' he said. 'Would you like some of my snack?' He held out a pot of grapes to Paul.

'Oh,' said Paul, 'thanks.'

Max was a new boy in their class. He'd moved here over the summer holidays. Paul took a couple of grapes from Max's pot and they looked around for Tim and Tom. But those two hadn't finished cleaning up yet.

Max asked: 'Are they always that stupid?'

Paul nodded. 'To me, at any rate. I'd better hide.'

He ran across the whole playground and then the sports field, to the gorse bushes right at the far end. There he crouched behind the largest bush and looked towards the

school. Max was watching him the whole time, and Paul signalled to him not to look over at him so obviously. He was so scared. Tim and Tom would be bound to get revenge once they'd finished clearing up. His heart was thumping in his throat. But he was secretly happy too. Finally. Proper vengeance at last. Thanks, Zippel, he thought.

Then he saw them. Tim and Tom were coming out of school. They were both searching, turning their heads. Tim gestured to Tom: *You go round to the left, I'll go right.* They ran slowly through the bustling playground, looking out for him. Three girls from their class laughed when they saw Tim. They turned their noses towards him and closed their eyes, sniffing as if he smelled particularly delicious. Tim took no notice but just kept scanning the playground with narrowed eyes. Paul's heart was in his mouth. At that moment, Tim pointed across the sports field towards him. Tom looked towards the bushes too, and nodded. They were both about to set off when, luckily, the bell rang. Tim and Tom looked at each other. They seemed to be considering whether they should run over to him anyway. But then they went back into the school. Max was the last at the glass door, and waved briefly to

show Paul that the coast was clear. But Paul still waited another minute before running back.

He just managed to slip back into the classroom on time so as not to miss the beginning of the next lesson. It was maths. Mr Ampermeier turned to the board.

'Righty-ho,' he said, writing up *17 + 25 + 6*. 'Let's see who's any good at mental arithmetic.'

He'd only just finished writing up the sum when Tim's voice shouted from the back: 'Mr Amplifier! Mr Amplifier! I know the answer, Mr Amplifier.'

Mr Ampermeier turned round, narrowed his eyes and looked sharply at Tim: 'I beg your pardon?' Mr Ampermeier always spoke extra quietly when he was angry.

Tim gulped. 'That wasn't me,' he said, 'I didn't say anything.'

Mr Ampermeier asked in that thin, cutting voice: 'Did you just call me Mr Amplifier?'

'No,' said Tim. 'Honest.'

Mr Ampermeier stood stock-still. His face flushed red and the veins in his neck were throbbing. Slowly, he turned back to the board.

At once, everyone could hear Tim's voice again: 'Mr

Amplifier, Mr Amplifier, I know what you get. Eleventy-hundred, seven thousand and twelvety lots of five.'

Tim shouted, even before Mr Ampermeier had finished turning round: 'Someone's copying my voice, Mr Ampli—sorry, Mr Ampermeier.'

'Oh really,' said Mr Ampermeier. 'And who can imitate your voice that well?'

'I . . . I . . . don't know,' stuttered Tim, looking questioningly at Tom, who looked equally baffled and was shaking his head frantically.

Out of the corner of his eye, Paul, who was desperately trying not to laugh, saw something white flitting over the ceiling.

Mr Ampermeier turned back to the board and was about to carry on writing.

'Hey, Mr Ampleliar, it was me.' This time it sounded as though Tom had called out.

Mr Ampermeier's hand stopped in mid-air, holding the chalk. For several long seconds. He looked like a waxwork except that the vein in his neck was so swollen you could see the blood throbbing through it. His whole face was red with fury.

'Ho ho,' said the voice, 'Ampleliar's angry head is such a pretty shade of red!'

Mr Ampermeier's whole body was trembling now. The chalk snapped in his fingers and he spoke extremely quietly: 'Get out, Tom! Now!'

Tom muttered that it hadn't been him, but Mr Ampermeier looked so formidable in his rage that he immediately stood up and walked out.

Mr Ampermeier was trying to calm down. He took several deep breaths, in and out, undid the top button of his shirt, looked briefly out of the window, then turned back to the board and said: 'Well, where was I? Oh, yes, *17 plus 25 plus 6*, what does that come to?'

He had just written the equals sign on the board when Tim's voice called out again: 'But Mr Campfire, what did you go and throw Tom out for?'

Mr Ampermeier froze. His right hand hovered by the board as the voice trilled:

A campfire can cook something yummy
To fill up your great big, fat tummy!

Mr Ampermeier turned as if in slow motion. His face was now lobster-pink, his neck was at full stretch, his eyes were almost bulging right out of his head. 'OUT!' he yelled. 'NOW!'

Tim ran in panic from the classroom.

After school, Paul rushed straight to the bike-shed in the car park. He was looking around nervously for Tim and Tom, but he couldn't see them in the crush. He kneeled down to unlock his bike, and when he looked up again, he saw the two of them by the school gate. Standing next to them were Mr Ampermeier and the head teacher who were both talking crossly to them. The boys looked much smaller than usual.

Paul jumped onto his bike and cycled slowly away. But he felt as though someone were pushing him along. As if he had the wind behind him. As if his bike were freewheeling all by itself. He pedalled and heard a very quiet voice singing in his school bag:

Eleventy-hundred, seven thousand, twelvety lots of three,

School is very boring, but it's over now, whoopee.
Eleventy-hundred, seven thousand, twelvety lots
  of four,
Timmy, Tommy, popple-pommy, they got shown
  the door.
Eleventy-hundred, seven thousand, twelvety lots
  of ten,
Tommy, Timmy, pipple-pimmy, daren't show up
  again.

Paul felt as though the voice was singing inside him. When he got to the stream, he stopped and just let his bike drop into the meadow. There was nobody in sight. Even before he'd taken his school bag off, Zippel came floating out.

'Whew,' grinned Paul, as he sat down in the grass.

'Whee-whew!' cried Zippel, doing a somersault in the air.

Paul beamed. 'That was so cool. I reckon they'll leave me alone now.'

'I should hope so,' said Zippel. 'Cos, well, school . . . Who on earth came up with an idea like that? Seventeen

and four, sixteen and five, and what's that tree called? I thought people played at school, like we do at home, only all together.'

'Nah, you have to sit quietly and learn stuff.'

'Oh,' said Zippel. 'I know lots already. Of course I'll come if you need me again, but if not, I think I'd rather stay at home and play waterfalls.'

At home. The words suddenly made Paul's whole body tense up. What if the lock had already been changed? After all, today was Friday. Paul gulped. He felt as though there was a cold, heavy lump in his stomach. He didn't want to spoil the happy mood, though, so he said nothing. Well. He said one thing: 'Hey, Zippel, thanks. You really did help me a lot.'

'Zigackly,' said Zippel. 'That's what I'm here for. Oh. What's the matter?'

Paul had suddenly fallen silent. No wonder. He'd spotted Tim. There he was, coming over the meadow on his orange bike. He wheeled very slowly over to the two of them, looking at Paul all the time. Paul stood up and wiped the grass off his hands. Zippel vanished behind the little tree that was right beside the stream. Tim parked his

bike near the tree. His school bag was strapped to the rack on the back. He came towards Paul without a word. Paul swallowed and forced himself not to run away. When Tim was a metre away, he said: 'You did that.'

'What?' asked Paul.

'With the yoghurt,' said Tim. 'And disguising your voice. I don't know how you did it, but it was all you.'

'Maybe,' said Paul, gulping again. 'But maybe it was someone else.'

'Oh, yeah?' scoffed Tim. 'And who would that be?'

'None of your business,' said Paul.

'Well,' said Tim. 'Do you know what's going to happen now?'

'Not a clue,' said Paul.

'Your school bag,' said Tim, pointing to Paul's school bag which lay on the grass between the two of them, 'is about to go for a swim down the stream. With all your books and pens and stuff. And doing funny voices won't help you then.'

'We'll see,' said Paul.

Tim hesitated. Paul was so different today. Normally, he was dead scared and stared at the ground as soon as

Tim spoke to him. But this time, Paul was facing him and just looking straight back. And because Paul was looking at him all the time, Tim didn't notice something small and white flitting rapidly beneath the saddle of his bike.

'Well,' said Paul. 'Do *you* know what's going to happen now?'

'You're just repeating what I said,' scoffed Tim. But he didn't sound as arrogant as usual, and he added: 'Why? What?'

'Your school bag,' said Paul, pointing over Tim's shoulder. 'And your bike. And the stream.'

Tim was really trying not to turn round, because that would be lame, obviously, but then he saw Paul smiling, and he heard a sound. Tyres, rolling through the grass. And when Tim *did* turn round, he saw his bike, ten metres away, gliding past him towards the stream. 'But . . .' he stammered, 'But . . . Stop!'

The bike kept rolling slowly on. Two ducks fluttered up in shock as it passed them. The bike was right on the edge now, another half metre and it would fall over the bank into the water.

'Stop!' called Paul. 'That's enough.'

The bike stopped, its front wheel dangling in the stream, its back wheel still on the meadow.

Tim stared wide-eyed at Paul. Then he slowly drew back. One step, two steps.

Paul stared calmly back. 'Just leave me in peace,' he said. 'OK?'

Tim ran to his bike. He grabbed it out of the stream, still staring at Paul, wrenched it round, leaped on and pedalled away so frantically, he almost fell off.

CHAPTER ELEVEN

Half an hour later, Paul was sitting in his bedroom when the doorbell rang. That must be Mr Nitzsche.

Paul's mum called from the kitchen: 'Paul? Can you get the door? I'm just in the middle of cooking.'

'OK.'

Zippel floated restlessly up and down in front of Paul. 'No!' he whispered. 'No-no-no. Let's just not open the door. Then the silly man will go away again. Or wait, I've got a better idea: I'll put a spell on him!' He hovered in the middle of the room, waved his arms around in the air and muttered:

Nasty Nitzsche, here's my spell:
You'll never-ever ring the bell.

It rang again.

'Paul?!' The voice from the kitchen was sounding impatient, although that might have something to do with a slight burning smell.

'Yes, yes, I'm coming,' said Paul.

Paul walked slowly down the hall and opened the door.

Standing in front of him was Mr Nitzsche with his enormous toolkit.

'Hi, Paul. I've come to . . . Oh, there's smoke coming from your kitchen. Is there a fire?'

'No, no, that's just Mum cooking,' said Paul.

'Oh, right,' said Mr Nitzsche. 'Anyway, I've come to change your lock.'

'Do you have to right now?' asked Paul. 'The old lock is still fine, actually.'

His mother appeared briefly in the kitchen doorway. 'Hello, Mr Nitzsche, good to see you.' There were little clouds of smoke following her. 'I need to start again; the spinach got a teeny-tiny bit burnt. Will you be all right getting on with it?'

'No problem,' said Mr Nitzsche.

He kneeled down by the open door and took a closer look at the lock, the screws, the door handle and the big keyhole. Finally, he shut his left eye and looked into it with his right. Suddenly he jerked his head back from the door and sucked air through his teeth, the way adults often do when something hurts and they don't want to say *ow*. 'Sugar! What the heck was that?' He was holding one hand over his right eye.

'What's the matter?' asked Paul.

'I don't know, said Mr Nitzsche. 'There was a cloud of dust. Could I wash my eye out, please?'

'Yes, of course,' said Paul, 'follow me.'

Paul opened the bathroom door, Mr Nitzsche bent over the washbasin and started carefully rinsing his eye with cold water.

At that very same moment, they heard an enormous noise that clattered and crashed right down the stairwell. Mr Nitzsche straightened up. Then there was another crash. Paul could see Mr Nitzsche's astonished expression in the mirror over the basin. They both listened. *Ding! Bang! Pow! Dong!* Mr Nitzsche ran out of the bathroom to the stairs with a dripping wet face. His toolbox was

no longer outside the door – it was up on the bannisters. And it was wide open. 'But . . .' he yelled, baffled. 'What on earth . . . ?'

He looked in the box. 'Where are my tools?' Then he leaned over the bannisters and looked down in disbelief.

'Holy moly . . . Who did that?' He looked up and down the stairs, then glared at Paul.

'It wasn't me,' said Paul, 'honest!'

Paul's mother appeared. 'What happened?'

'Somebody threw my tools down the stairs.'

'What? Paul, was it you?'

'No, honestly it wasn't, I'd never do anything like that, and anyway, I was showing you the bathroom.'

'Yes, that's true,' said Mr Nitzsche.

'Ouch! What happened to your eye?' asked Paul's mother in horror.

The eye was looking pretty bad – it was red and watering, as if Mr Nitzsche had rubbed onion juice into it.

'No idea,' he said. 'I was just looking into your lock when all this dust blew into my eye. I think I'll pop to the

doctor's. It stings a bit. Is it OK if I change your lock on Monday instead?'

'Yes, of course,' said Paul's mum.

'I'll help you pick up your tools,' offered Paul, slowly following Mr Nitzsche down the stairs.

CHAPTER TWELVE

Over tea, Paul's mum asked: 'How on earth did all those tools tumble down like that?'

'No idea,' said Paul.

'There really wasn't anyone on the stairs?'

'Well, I guess there must have been,' said Paul. He pushed the bone-dry cauliflower around his plate a bit.

'Who, though?' said his mum.

Instead of answering, Paul asked: 'Anyway, what are we doing at the weekend?'

'Oh, no idea, how about a trip somewhere?'

'Ooh, yes!' cried Paul.

'Hmm,' said Mum. 'What's up with you?'

'Why?'

'Well, normally if I say "Let's go on a trip," you react

as if I've told you to tidy your room.' She screwed her face up until she looked all frowny and grumpy, and put on a sulky voice: "Do we have to? I don't want to. I'd rather stay here."'

'Yeah. Uh, no. Um . . .' Paul thought for a moment and then said: 'I really urgently need to look at a castle.'

'A castle?'

'Yes. A castle. You know, where kings and knights used to live. Like last year in Italy, where there was even still that drawbridge.'

'Oh, you mean the *Castello di Uviglie*,' sighed Mum, with the strange look on her face that she always got when she was remembering something nice.

'Don't remember the name,' said Paul.

'Ah, that was suuuch a beautiful place,' gushed Mum. 'The gardens. The paintings. And do you remember, in the evening we sat in the piazza in that little village and—'

'Exactly,' Paul interrupted. 'There must be a castle like that somewhere round here too.'

'Yes, of course,' said Paul's mum. 'Castle Grafenburg. We went there once with you, when you were two.' She got that look on her face again. 'You stomped down all

the long corridors on your little legs and said: "I want to live here." Do you remember?' She looked fondly at Paul.

'No, not at all, but it's even better that way. Can we go there, please? Please!'

'Of course,' said his mum.

'Tomorrow?' Paul asked at once.

'Fine by me,' said Mum.

'Promise?' asked Paul.

'Yes, sure,' said Mum. 'Promise. But why's it so urgent?'

'For school,' he lied. 'Because we're reading something about knights and castles. But I've got homework to do now.'

He went to his room, but then turned back again: 'It's really hard stuff, Mum, I really need to contemplate, so I'm shutting the door, OK?'

Mum laughed quietly and said: 'It is important to *concentrate*, so you just shut your door.'

Paul shut his door behind him and ran over to the toy shop.

'Hey, come out,' he whispered into the till.

No reaction.

Paul looked in the bookcase. Nothing. He looked at

the train set, he looked under his bed, he looked in his wardrobe drawers, but Zippel was nowhere. Paul went into the hallway, crept past the kitchen door and looked into the keyhole of the flat door. Nothing to be seen.

'Hey, are you in here?' he whispered, and pressed his ear to the door, but it was perfectly silent. In the end, he went to his parents' bedroom and glanced into all the drawers in their wardrobe. But Zippel remained missing.

'What are you doing in here?' His mother was standing in the bedroom doorway.

'Oh,' said Paul, 'nothing, I was just looking for my green jumper.'

'The green jumper you're wearing?' Mum crossed her arms.

Paul looked down at himself. Rats.

His mother frowned at him. 'Weren't you going to do your homework?'

'Oh, yes, bother, so I was,' said Paul as if he'd only forgotten for a moment, and he went back to his room and closed the door.

CHAPTER THIRTEEN

A little later, the doorbell rang. Paul ran straight to the hallway to open the door, but his mother beat him to it. Standing in the stairwell was Mr Nitzsche. There was a kind of bandage over his right eye, white and thick.

'Oh dear, how's your eye?' asked Paul's mum.

'Oh, that,' said Mr Nitzsche, carefully touching the bandage. 'Not so bad. One of the little veins burst. I have to wear this plaster for a couple of days, then it'll all be fine. But . . .' Mr Nitzsche stood there, looking properly confused.

'What's wrong?' asked Paul's mum.

'I don't know myself,' said Mr Nitzsche, scratching his head. 'Well . . . In my flat . . . '

Paul's mother frowned. 'What's the matter?'

116

'You'll have to see for yourself,' said Mr Nitzsche as he hurried down the stairs again.

'Can I come too?' asked Paul.

'Fine by me,' called Mr Nitzsche from the half-landing.

Mum picked up her door key and pulled the door shut behind her and they both followed Mr Nitzsche down the stairs, across the yard and up to the second floor again on the other side. Mr Nitzsche was muttering away to himself all the time as he climbed the stairs ahead of them. His door was open. He took a step back, stretched out his arm in welcome and said: 'Please, after you.'

Paul and his mum walked down the hall into the little living room. There was a large bookcase there.

'Oh,' said Mum, 'what a fun idea.' She pointed at the books, which were all sorted by colour. Right at the top were the ones with a white spine, then a few shelves of red ones, then green, a few blues, and so on.

'Do you think so?' said Mr Nitzsche, looking at the books. 'Well, maybe it is fun – but it wasn't my idea.'

'What do you mean?' asked Paul's mum.

'Before I went to the doctor's earlier, the books were all jumbled up. When I came back, they were sorted by colour.'

'Oh, really?' said Paul's mum. 'Does anyone else live here?'

'Not that I know of!' said Mr Nitzsche. 'And the bookcase is just the start.' He went into his bedroom and opened his wardrobe. In one pile were red jumpers, T-shirts and socks. In another pile were blue jeans and a few blue shirts and T-shirts.

Paul's mum couldn't help laughing quietly.

'You laugh,' said Mr Nitzsche, 'but coming home to your own flat and finding everything different is pretty creepy.'

'Everything?' asked Paul. 'Is *everything* sorted so weirdly?'

Mr Nitzsche nodded. 'The towels in the bathroom. My store cupboard . . . I like making jam, you know – everything's sorted strictly by colour. You've seen the wardrobe – now come and have a look in the kitchen.'

Paul ran to the kitchen. Everything looked pretty normal. Until Mr Nitzsche opened the crockery cupboard. There were the white plates and cups – and next to them was white yoghurt, a piece of white feta cheese, milk, hankies, white candles. The mug cupboard had a couple

of red cups beside the tomatoes, and there were two oranges and some orange napkins in an orange bowl.

'Someone wanted to tidy up for you,' said Paul's mum.

'Yes, but who?' asked Mr Nitzsche. 'I live alone here. And nobody but me has a key. I think I ought to call the police.'

'The police?!' cried Paul, immediately realising that he'd shouted far too loudly.

Mr Nitzsche looked at him. 'Well, yes, there's been a break-in here.'

Paul's mum nodded. 'True. But nothing's gone missing, has it? Couldn't it have been children, playing a trick on you?'

'Or . . . or wanting to say sorry for something?' said Paul.

'I tell you what,' said Paul's mum. 'How about I just help you put things straight again?'

'And I'll get back to my homework,' said Paul. 'Bye, Mr Nitzsche.'

He just heard Mr Nitzsche saying to Mum: 'When I change your lock on Monday, I'll change mine too.

This one's really old as well. And I'll look round the whole house to see who else has a lock like this that's easy to pick.'

Paul ran quickly back to the main house. He'd hardly got the flat door open before he called out: 'Zippel! Come out at once! Where are you?'

Zippel seemed to be waiting for him. He was floating above the carpet in the middle of the room, beaming. 'Well, was he pleased?'

'You must be kidding!' cried Paul.

Zippel paused for a moment, then he said: 'No, you're the kid around here, not me.'

'I mean: you're nuts!'

'No, I'm not,' said the ghost, still smiling. 'I share my lock, I mean your door, with a really teeny-weeny spider called Alan, but I definitely haven't got any nuts in there—'

'Hey,' Paul interrupted him. 'You went into Mr Nitzsche's flat.'

'Yes, zigackly, I did,' said Zippel proudly. 'And I tidied up sooooo neatly! Really truly.' Zippel flitted excitedly to

and fro, waggling his little arms in the air and singing:

When everything is in a mess,
Mr Nitzsche's in a stress.
When everything is in its place,
Mr Nitzsche's feeling ace.

'Oh no, he's not,' cried Paul. 'Mr Nitzsche almost called the police because of you. He thinks it was burglars. On Monday he'll definitely change your lock. And all the other old locks in the house along with it.'

Zippel sank down to the carpet. 'What? Why? Oh no. Oh nooooo. I didn't want that.'

He started to sob.

'Boohoohoohoo, I wanted to exscreeeeeews myself. For hurting his eye. And now . . . I get everything wrong.'

Paul sighed. His whole carpet was covered in cobwebs of dusty tears again. And he was almost in tears himself when he said: 'Guess what, tomorrow we're going to a proper castle.'

'What's a proper castle?' sniffed Zippel, wiping a few teary threads from his face.

'Um, one for kings and princesses.'

'Oh,' said Zippel. 'Aha. But . . . but you're going too?'

'Yes, of course,' said Paul, trying to smile. 'Don't worry. I'll take you there.'

'You'll take me there? What do you mean? Are you going away again?'

'We'll look at it. And if you like it, you can stay there.'

The ghost started to cry again. 'Boohoohoohoooo. You're leeeeeeeaving me! I'm a baaad ghost.'

When Paul saw him like that, he didn't know whether to laugh or to cry too. Dear, dear Zippel, he thought. He was so fond of him. He'd probably never liked anybody as much as this little white creature that was currently spreading cobweb tears around the whole room.

'Oh, Zippel,' he said, 'you're a super ghost. But you're a keyhole ghost. I think you'd be better off in an old castle lock. Not just the door to a little flat. A lock in a big, old castle with towers and spiral staircases and treasure chests and suits of armour. Where there are other ghosts haunting the corridors at night.'

'Hunting?' asked Zippel, wiping away more dusty tears from his face. 'What do they hunt? Doesn't it mess up the corridors?'

'Haunting,' said Paul. 'They float through the corridors at night, making spooky noises.'

'How do you know all that stuff?' asked Zippel.

'It's in all the ghost stories.' Paul went to his bookcase and pulled three books off the shelves. They all showed a small ghost hovering over a castle. 'Look,' said Paul. 'They all live in big, old-fashioned knightly castles.'

'Uh-huh,' said Zippel, not really convinced. 'And who wrote them?'

'Um, lots of authors.'

'What does that mean? Are they ghosts?'

'No, authors are people. They're grown-ups who write books.'

'Grow-nups!' yelled Zippel, outraged. 'Grow-nups! What do grow-nups know about ghosts? They know nothing! Nothing! Grow-nups are all stupid and big and stick keys in my lock and take lovely old locks out of doors and put ugly new locks in and complain and make things silly and tidy with colours while other grow-nups make things tidy with no colours and they're all cross all the time! Really truly!'

'Yes, but do you know the good thing about a castle?' said Paul. 'A proper castle? There are no grown-ups in the evenings and at night.'

'Oh,' said Zippel. 'Really? Not even one?'

'Not one. At night you can be as noisy as you like. And there's lots of dirt and dust and antique doors with even antiquer locks in them.'

'Oh,' said Zippel. 'Where's this castle with no grow-nups then?'

'You'll see. We'll go tomorrow.'

'Mm. And these authors, what do they write about ghosts?'

'That they rattle their chains. And float down corridors going *wooo* and *boo!* and live in armour and spend the nights in treasure chests.'

'There, you see,' said Zippel. 'Your authors haven't a clue. I'm a real ghost. And the ones in your books are only drawings. But, fine, let's go and have a look. Really truly. Sometimes you're almost as strange as a grow-nup.'

CHAPTER FOURTEEN

When Paul and his parents left the house the next morning, they paused by the letter boxes. A large sheet of paper had been stuck up. In rather scribbly writing, it said:

Dear Mr Nitsha
Ime very sory, very, very.
Your the bestest bestest caretaker Ive ever met.
And I hope your eye gets better soon.
Ime very sory about that to. Reely truly.
I did it all rong.
But now Ime going away and it will all be good.
Hopefuly. An it wasnt Pauls fault. Promiss!
Yours sinceerly,
A stranger hoo you dont no

127

Paul's mum laughed. 'Someone seems to have a guilty conscience.'

'And very bad spelling,' said Paul's dad.

Paul said nothing.

Then they set off. Mum told them that she'd booked a tour online for ten o'clock, and how happy she was that they were all going out together, and how nervous she was about her opera performance. Dad hardly said a word, again.

Paul was very quiet too. He'd brought his little rucksack, which he held tightly with both hands, keeping it in his lap all the way. He spent most of the time looking out of the window, and swallowing down the sadness that rose up inside him whenever he thought about what would happen with Zippel and the castle.

They arrived at the castle just before ten. When Mum saw that Paul was bringing his rucksack, she said: 'You can leave that in the car if you like.'

'No,' said Paul, 'I'm bringing it with me.'

'But why?'

'Because,' said Paul, hugging the rucksack tight. There

would normally have been a long discussion, but Mum was determined not to miss the tour. So she shrugged and said: 'Fine, bring it then.'

When they got to the entrance, Paul had quite a shock: there was a security guard in a grey uniform, checking all the bags.

The man gave Paul a fierce look and said: 'Open that up!'

'The rucksack?' asked Paul.

'Yes, obviously the rucksack, what else?'

'It's only got a snack in it,' said Paul.

'Doesn't matter. The mayor's visiting today so we have to check every bag and every visitor,' said the guard.

He took the rucksack from Paul, took out the flask without a word, and shook it. Then he held it to his ear and shook it more violently.

'Not so hard!' cried Paul.

'There's no tea in it,' said the guard.

'I drank it on the way because it was such a long journey,' mumbled Paul.

'Hmm,' said the guard, tipping it from side to side again.

Then he said: 'OK.'

Paul shoved the flask back into the bag and ran after his parents.

A big man in a black suit was standing on the wide castle staircase. A group of people were waiting around him. That must be the tour.

'I need to go to the loo,' cried Paul, heading for the gents. 'You go on, I'll find you.'

As soon as he reached the toilets, he opened the rucksack, took out the flask and unscrewed the lid.

'Phew,' he said, 'that was close.'

'Pheeew,' groaned Zippel, deep inside the flask. 'That wasn't close. That was an earthquake. Or the cola-roaster at the Novemberfest.'

'Roller-coaster,' said Paul. 'Oktoberfest. Come on, quickly, we're here.'

Zippel floated out, but he swayed to and fro, to and fro, over the flask, like steam snaking up from a cup of hot tea. 'I'm still all wibble-wobble-wibbly dizzy,' he groaned.

'I'm sorry,' said Paul. 'But I've got to go on this tour. Are you coming? You'll be able to see the castle then.'

'Fine by me,' said Zippel.

'Just make sure nobody sees you,' Paul called as he ran off. But Zippel had long since floated up to the ceiling and, very handily, he was exactly the same shade of white as most of the walls, so he was pretty much invisible floating along up there.

When Paul got back to the entrance hall, the group was still standing on the stairs. The man in the black suit had a name badge on his jacket. It said: Dr Schlomm. He had a very loud voice and an even louder laugh, and he kept glancing over to a woman in a green skirt. Paul asked his mother what was going on.

'Oh,' sighed Mum, 'the woman over there, the one in the green skirt, is the mayor of Grafenburg. She is going to join the tour. And the castle manager keeps on telling her how efficient and brilliant he is.'

At that moment, Dr Schlomm clapped his big hands and said: 'Okaaay. Wonderful, all good, let's get going then.'

He took the group down a long corridor, staying by the mayor's side all the time, and explained that the whole castle used to look dreadful. 'When I started as manager here, it was practically derelict,' he said, 'but I've had every room renovated over the past five years. And now – it's wonderful, all improved. You won't find a single speck of dust or rust anywhere in the castle any more. All spotless.'

He was just saying that the building works had cost six million euros when a little girl with red plaits and black glasses interrupted: 'Are there any ghosts here in the castle?'

Dr Schlomm was apparently not used to being interrupted. He stood there for a moment, staring at the girl open-mouthed. Then he said: 'Of course not. There are no such things as ghosts. Not here and not anywhere else.'

He shook his head in annoyance. Then he walked on, telling the mayor that he'd had all the old doors and locks changed for ultra-modern fire doors and that that had also been very expensive. 'But now – security locks everywhere, wonderful, all good.'

Paul groaned quietly when he heard that about the security locks.

The girl with the red plaits interrupted again. 'Excuse me, Dr Schlomm, but how do you know there's no such thing as ghosts?'

The manager stopped in the middle of the corridor, as if frozen to the spot. Then he said, rather loudly: 'Let's keep things nice and polite, shall we? If you children have

any questions, kindly put up your hands.'

Bang. At the same moment, a suit of armour fell over at the end of the corridor; the helmet rolled slowly across the wooden floor. It looked as though someone had chopped the armour's head off.

Dr Schlomm ran off anxiously down the corridor. 'Oh, my goodness. That's from the fourteenth century. A particularly valuable piece from our collection. Could someone help me, please?'

The mayor kneeled down, she and Dr Schlomm grabbed the suit of armour and put it back upright again. Paul, who had run over with them, was about to pick up the helmet when the manager bent down beside him and hissed: 'Hands off. I'll do that myself.'

As Dr Schlomm picked up the helmet with both hands and straightened up with it, his own voice spoke quietly from the helmet: 'Let's keep things nice and polite, shall we?'

Dr Schlomm was so startled that he accidentally stood on the mayor's foot.

'Oh, excuse me,' he said, 'I'm terribly sorry.'

'Oh, exscrews me,' whispered the helmet, 'me too, most

tebberly sorry,' but nobody heard it except Dr Schlomm, and Paul, who was standing beside him.

Paul had to laugh. Dr Schlomm looked in confusion from the helmet to Paul and back again. Paul could tell that Dr Schlomm would have dearly loved to yell at him, but for one thing, Paul hadn't done anything and, for another, the whole group had gathered around him and the armour again.

So Dr Schlomm set the helmet cautiously onto the suit of armour, smoothed his tie and said: 'Well, that went well. Wonderful, all good. So, let's go to the ceremonial hall. Mrs Mayor, if you'd kindly follow me.'

The mayor rolled her eyes slightly as the manager fluttered so anxiously around her again.

Paul's mum, who was standing right next to her, whispered to the mayor: 'It seems to me that the manager's doing the whole tour just for you.'

The mayor whispered back: 'I get that impression too. It's terribly embarrassing. It must be because he wants more money for building work. He's always writing me letters about how he needs more and more.'

Dr Schlomm hurried along at the head of the group.

Paul was now walking beside the red-haired girl who had asked about ghosts. They smiled at each other.

'This Schlomm has no idea,' the girl said quietly.

Dr Schlomm was just stopping in a smaller room with all kinds of golden plates, from large serving platters to small saucers, on the walls. He rubbed his hands enthusiastically: 'So, ladies and gentlemen, Mrs Mayor, this is the royal dining room. I have had our extraordinarily valuable collection of plates displayed here.'

The girl put up her hand. Dr Schlomm pretended at first that he hadn't seen her, and he just kept talking until the mayor said: 'I think this young lady has a question.'

Dr Schlomm put on a wry smile and said: 'Weeell, my dear, what would you like to know?'

'I wanted to ask again about the gho—'

'Little girl!' Dr Schlomm interrupted her, 'there are no flying saucers, no unicorns and there are certainly no gho—'

He was obviously about to say 'ghosts', but at that very moment he saw, behind the group of visitors, one of the golden saucers detach itself very gently from the wall and float slowly across the room towards the door.

Paul, his parents, the mayor and all the other visitors had their backs to the plates. They just saw Dr Schlomm turn as white as chalk. His mouth opened and closed in slow motion. And then he stammered: 'A flying . . . a flying . . . the saucer, um, it really is highly, highly valuable.'

By the time the group turned round, the small golden plate had already floated out of the room into the hallway and there was nothing to be seen but a wall of large and small plates.

'What do you mean?' asked the mayor. 'What's the matter with you?'

Dr Schlomm sank down onto a golden throne, staring silently into space. The visitors looked at him in concern. But Paul and the girl ran out of the room into the corridor. The only thing there was a table. On it stood a single plate. Paul spotted Zippel flitting round the corner at the far end of the hallway as the girl asked him: 'Do you believe in ghosts too?'

Paul said: 'Hm, well, maybe, but I can't imagine any ghosts living in a castle like this one.'

CHAPTER FIFTEEN

When Paul and the girl returned to the hall, Dr Schlomm was standing in the middle of the group once more, saying: 'Wonderful, all good. I just needed to catch my breath for a moment. Now I'd like to show you, Mrs Mayor, the three most beautiful rooms in the castle.'

So he walked through the halls, telling them how great they were now and how dreadfully expensive the repairs had been, by which time, some of the adults were shaking their heads at his stupid tour.

Meanwhile, Zippel had discovered something much, much more exciting. After hiding behind the plate and floating out of the dining hall with it, he had flown all alone down the long corridor and disappeared round the

nearest corner into a little side passage. There, he stopped for a moment in mid-air, whispering: 'Ooooooohh . . .'

Until then, Zippel had found everything in the castle so ugly – no rust, no dust, no oil, and all the locks were brand-new and tiny. But this passage, now, this was something else! There was the bright-red barrier tape for a start. That looked really interesting. The tape had big shouty warning letters on it. To Zippel, that looked even more interesting.

He hovered cautiously in the semi-darkness. Cobwebs everywhere. And dust. Lots of dust. On the floor. On the walls. On the ceiling. There were a few planks lying around, tools, spades and bricks, all higgledy-piggledy. But best of all, Zippel thought, it was lovely and dark. The old window shutters were almost completely closed so only a few milky-white strips of light could find their way in. After a few metres, there was another corner. Round it stood a wonky throne with its left armrest missing. A little further on, there were picture frames on the wall. Zippel floated deeper into the darkness, past a rusty suit of armour and a few lances and swords.

And then he saw the clock. An old, heavy grandfather clock with a long, chunky pendulum chain. Zippel

immediately started to swing the chain to and fro. Unfortunately, it was so rusty it snapped in the middle. By now, Zippel was really excited. It looked just like the chains that Paul had told him about, the ones in his castle-ghost-books. The chains that the ghosts rattled when they haunted corridors. He picked up the chain, wrapped it around himself once, twice, like a scarf, and flew down the dark corridor with it.

'Hoo-boo, boo-hoo!' he cried. Then he swung the chain with both hands, shouting in a deep voice: 'Rattle, rattle, rattle.' He chased little clouds of dust to his left and to his right, crying: 'I'm a hunting ghost!', and hunted, rattled and woohoo-booed his way down the passage. He was having such a good time that he made up a little hunting and haunting song:

Rattle, rattle, boo-di-hoo.
I'm so scary, shoo-bi-doo.
Boo-di-hoo and rattle-run,
Hunting is enormous fun!

CHAPTER SIXTEEN

There was something that Zippel couldn't know, however: the dark passageway he was enjoying so much led directly to the coronation hall. The very same coronation hall where Dr Schlomm, the mayor and the group of visitors had just arrived. Dr Schlomm was in the middle of telling them that all the lamps had been replaced the month before, and how exceptionally expensive that had been, when a sudden series of very strange noises could be heard in one corner of the hall.

Paul noticed a door marked: 'Strictly no entry! Building site!' The noise seemed to be coming from behind that door. It sounded as though someone was bashing on the strings of a guitar with a hammer, as an accompaniment to a very peculiar song. Or was that just

the wind, howling in through a gutter?

Dr Schlomm froze. 'Please wait for me here, I'd better take a look.' He opened the door and vanished behind it.

Before he could close it again, however, Paul slipped through with him. Dr Schlomm was about to tell him off, but his mouth just hung open. Floating right in front of him was a ghost. As clear as day. A glowing, white ghost with a rattling chain, rocking to and fro in the middle of the room, tossing its head furiously and, even worse, singing hideously off-key.

In the meantime, you see, Zippel had found an old and very out-of-tune harp, standing between a couple of tables.

He was clattering up and down the strings with his rattly chain, running it back and forth, forth and back, *ker-plong-plonk-plonk, ker-pling-ling-ling*, and it all sounded seriously skewed and distorted, even without his little song, which he was still singing. It had been adapted from a haunting and hunting song into a haunting and taunting song, though, and it went like this:

Rattle-rittle-ruttle-rastle,
Someone's spoilt this lovely castle.
Boo-di-hoo and hoo-di-bom,
You're the fool, old Dr Schlomm.

'WHAT A CHEEK!' a voice suddenly screamed from behind Zippel. The ghost jumped so violently that he dropped the chain right onto the harp strings, and the noise was awful. But even worse, there was an enormous grow-nup standing there: the horrible Dr Schlomm.

Dr Schlomm's face was red with rage and he began roaring: 'Security! Cleaners! Police! All hands on deck! What a messss!!'

Zippel was panicking and looking around the corridor for somewhere to hide when he spotted Paul behind

Dr Schlomm's back. Paul whipped his flask out of his rucksack, unscrewed the lid, and waved it invitingly.

Dr Schlomm had his eyes shut as he screamed: 'Clean this up at once! Everything out! Get rid of the dust and dirt! I want every last scrap gone by tomorrow morning.'

Dr Schlomm was roaring so blindly he didn't even see Zippel whoosh past him and vanish into Paul's flask.

By this time, the tour party had opened the door from the hall. For a while, they all looked on in amazement as Dr Schlomm stood in the cluttered passageway, yelling at chairs and tables.

Eventually, the mayor said: 'Excuse me, Dr Schlomm, but all these people have made rather long journeys to come on your tour. Would you kindly now tell us something interesting about this castle for a change, instead of either showing off or having tantrums?'

'No,' said Dr Schlomm, still bright red in the face. 'This tour is over. Goodbye.' And with that, he vanished down the dark hallway towards his office.

The group stood flabbergasted around the door, watching him go.

Only Paul heard the red-haired girl whisper: 'They so do exist.'

The first visitors were about to head out of the coronation hall towards the exit when somebody suddenly spoke: 'Uh, if you like . . . '

Paul turned towards the voice. It was his dad. He was standing in the middle of the group and saying: 'I know quite a lot about history, and I could give you a bit of a tour – it would be a shame if you all just had to go home now.'

The others looked at each other in amazement. A few hesitated for a moment, but Paul's dad rubbed his hands, coughed twice and began: 'OK, so. It was like this: King Kunibert the Proud died here, in this hall where we're standing, after the Battle of Waldofing. He died of a terrible sword injury that he'd suffered while fighting Bertram the Most Abominable . . . '

And Dad told stories: about Kunibert and his golden sword. About the terrible Battle of Waldofing. And about Kunibert's great golden treasure that is said to lie hidden somewhere beneath the castle to this day. Now things were properly interesting, and people listened in fascination.

146

Paul was amazed at how much his dad knew, and by the time they reached the entrance again, an hour had passed and everyone was clapping.

Once the applause had died down, the mayor stepped out of the tour party and said: 'Thank you very much – you saved the day for us all. As mayor, I'm in overall charge of everyone who works here at the castle. I'm sure you have enough to do with your work and your family, but if you ever wanted to lead tours here again, I'd be very pleased to welcome you.'

'Really?!' cried Dad, grabbing the mayor's hand. 'When can I start?'

Mum looked at him in surprise. The mayor looked at him in surprise, and Paul looked at him in surprise.

'Uh, well, tomorrow, if you like,' said the mayor.

'Done,' said Dad, shaking the mayor's hand so vigorously that the sleeves of her blouse fluttered madly.

'But . . .' said Mum.

'I'll be here at ten o'clock tomorrow,' cried Dad.

'But . . .' said Paul.

Dad looked at him and Mum and said: 'The three of

us should head to the café; there's something I should have told you a long time ago.'

And so, five minutes later, they were sitting on the terrace outside the museum café. At first, Dad stared at the car park because he didn't know where to start. And actually the car park was really very interesting, just then. Dr Schlomm was standing there, still bright red in the face, ordering the two police officers who'd answered his call to kindly get on with arresting the ghost in his castle. The two police officers looked at each other, and then enquired politely if Dr Schlomm might not be feeling a little feverish.

And just as Paul's dad was finally about to say something, an ambulance drove up. A doctor got out and talked soothingly to Dr Schlomm.

Eventually, Paul's mum said: 'Come on, spit it out – what's bothering you?'

So Paul's dad looked at them both, gulped twice and said: 'I lost my job a few days ago.'

Paul's mum lowered her cake fork and stopped chewing so that you could see the crumbs of chocolate cake in her mouth.

Dad told them that since the beginning of the week, a computer had been doing his job, so that he wasn't needed any more, and that he'd only be paid for another month.

'But you're a teacher,' said Paul.

'Well,' said Paul's dad. 'I'm a bit like a teacher. I teach new recruits in our company how to write computer programs, but they're all meant to teach themselves now.'

'But why didn't you say anything?' asked Paul's mum.

'I wanted to, all the time,' said Paul's dad. 'But I didn't know how. And you've got your performance next week so I didn't want to add to your worries.'

'And you've spent a lot of time sitting around at home, haven't you?' asked Paul.

'How do you know that?' asked Paul's dad.

'Oh, just because,' said Paul mysteriously.

'Yes . . . every day,' Dad went on. 'I've been searching for new jobs on the internet.' Then he smiled and said: 'And instead, I've found one here, by chance. A little one, at any rate. For the time being. And history, knights, the

Middle Ages, castles – all that stuff was always far more interesting than stupid computers.' Only dad used a ruder word than 'stupid'.

'Language!' said Paul and his mum at the same time, and laughed.

CHAPTER SEVENTEEN

When they got home two hours later, Paul went straight to his room. He'd barely opened the flask when Zippel came shooting out like a ping-pong ball.

He shook himself out in the air to his proper size and immediately starting complaining: 'Awful. Aaaaaawful!'

'What is?' asked Paul.

'Everything!' shouted Zippel, so loudly that Paul hissed at him to talk more quietly.

'Everything,' repeated Zippel in a whisper. 'That pitch-black flask. Driving around in that pitch-black flask. Sitting around for ever in the café in that pitch-black flask.'

'Sorry,' said Paul, 'but I had to get you to the castle and back somehow, didn't I?'

'Zigackly!' shouted Zippel furiously. 'The castle.

That was the awfulest thing of all. What grow-nup had the idea that ghosts could live in stone boxes like that? Total nonsense. Keyhole ghosts need a cosy little lock, not a massive, clean and tidy box. Dr Screamy-Schlomm. Bah! I'm never going there again. Never! Do you hear me?'

'Yes,' said Paul quietly. 'I'm not deaf. It was probably a stupid idea of mine. But now I really don't know what we're going to do.'

Paul looked very sad, sitting there hunched and puzzled on his bed.

Zippel immediately floated over and patted his knee.

'Oh, it'll work out,' he said. 'Don't worry. Really truly.'

'Yeah?' asked Paul.

'Course,' said Zippel. 'If you don't know what to do, a friendly ghost will help you too. Old ghostly saying, just invented by Zippel the Very First.'

At that moment, there was a knock on Paul's door. Zippel whizzed up to the ceiling. Paul's mum opened the door. She was holding the phone and looking rather confused. 'Mrs Wilhelm would like to speak to you.'

Paul gulped. Mrs Wilhelm. Why could she be phoning? Had she just told his parents that he'd broken into her flat? Paul took the telephone and said quietly: 'Hello?'

'Is that Paul?' asked Mrs Wilhelm.

'Yes,' said Paul.

'Hello, Paul, this is Mrs Wilhelm speaking. Would you pop up and see me, please?'

'Uh, now?' asked Paul.

'Yes, if you have time.'

Paul tried to answer as calmly as possible. 'That's fine,' he said, hanging up.

'What does Mrs Wilhelm want?' asked Mum.

'No idea,' said Paul, putting on his shoes. He was trembling so much, he could hardly tie the laces. Without looking round, he called, 'Back in a bit,' and went out. Boy, oh boy. What on earth did she want? But it was still better for her to scold him than to come down and tell his parents. He walked slowly up the stairs. They creaked with every step. Three floors is quite a lot of steps when you're afraid of what's waiting for you up above. He'd got to the top and was about to ring the bell when he saw that Mrs Wilhelm's door was open a crack.

'Come in,' she called from inside when he knocked cautiously.

Paul pushed open the creaky door. The hall was empty. There was a light on, down in the sitting room. Everywhere else was dark. Hesitantly, he walked down the narrow passage. In the dark, the empty picture frames looked even creepier than they did in the daytime.

'Hellooo?' he enquired in the darkness.

'I'm in the sitting room,' called Mrs Wilhelm's croaky voice.

Paul gulped. The old wooden floorboards creaked. In the kitchen, the tap was dripping, drop, drop, drop. Three more steps, and he was standing at the sitting room door. Mrs Wilhelm was sitting in the armchair where he'd sat last time. She was looking at the shelves with all the locks, although Paul couldn't see if she was really looking at the bookcase. From the side like this, he could only see her strangely-squinting left eye, which seemed even more wrinkled than normal.

'Come in,' she said, pointing at the second chair, 'and sit here with me.'

Paul walked round Mrs Wilhelm and sat in the old

 154

armchair. Now she turned her head slowly towards him, stared at him with her one large eye and asked: 'Well? Did you come alone?'

'Er, yes,' said Paul with a gulp. 'Why? Should I have brought my parents?'

Suddenly the idea of his parents being here seemed very attractive. 'Shall I run and fetch them?' he asked, on the point of jumping up.

Mrs Wilhelm laughed quietly. 'Certainly not! Stay where you are.' She reached out her bony hand to stop him standing up. 'The two of us need to talk alone.'

Paul sat stiff as a board. Mrs Wilhelm pointed to the little table between the two chairs. There was a small bowl filled with black balls. 'Would you like one?' she asked.

'No, thank you,' said Paul. Was she trying to poison him? Mrs Wilhelm took one of the balls herself and bit it in half. 'I always used to eat these chocolates with my husband,' she said.

'Thanks,' said Paul, 'but we'll be having dinner soon.'

Mrs Wilhelm looked at him again. Perhaps her eye only looked so big because the other one was always squinting. She fixed her healthy blue eye on him, said nothing at all for what must have been ten seconds, and then asked: 'What's its name, then?'

'What?' asked Paul. 'Who?'

'Come on,' said Mrs Wilhelm, 'I may be *really* old, but I'm not *really* stupid.'

Paul gulped. He felt trapped. To win a bit of time, he asked: 'What actually happened to your eye?'

'Well,' Mrs Wilhelm asked in return, 'what happened to Mr Nitzsche's eye?'

'Oh, that,' said Paul, 'that's different. He hurt it when he was looking into our lock yesterday.'

'Yes, exactly,' said Mrs Wilhelm, 'that's what he told me. And whether you believe it or not, something very similar happened to me. Except that it was seventy-five years ago. On the 10th of August. I'll never forget that because it was the worst day of my life. And the best.'

'Why?' asked Paul. 'What happened?'

'I was about your age,' said Mrs Wilhelm. 'Eight years old. And I lived with my parents in the ground-floor flat.'

'Really?' said Paul, who didn't know himself which he found more surprising: that Mrs Wilhelm had once been as young as he was, or that she'd lived in this building since she was a child.

As if she'd heard his thoughts, Mrs Wilhelm said: 'I was even born here. But that's another story. At any rate, I had my own door key. Just like you. My parents had a little shop. We sold buttons and braces, sewing things and fabric. My parents worked all day, but we still had hardly any money. Sometimes there was only milk for supper, and nothing to eat. But that's another story too.'

She popped the second half of the chocolate into her mouth, closed her good eye and chewed it slowly and

lingeringly, without saying a word. She seemed to be really savouring it. Then she rubbed her hands together and said: 'Anyway, I came home from school one afternoon and heard a funny noise as I was about to unlock the door. It sounded as though someone was talking inside the door. When I looked into the keyhole, there was a sudden cloud of dust and rust. And there must have been a little piece of metal in there too. I didn't pull my head away quickly enough. There weren't such good doctors in those days as there are now and so I lost my left eye. But I gained a friend in return. Maybe the best friend I ever had.'

She looked at Paul with her blue eye and said quietly, as if she were telling him a secret: 'His name was Quockle.'

'Quockle?' asked Paul. 'Quockle? What kind of a name is that?'

'Well, when he was rattling around in the lock, rabbiting on to himself, it sounded like "quockle-quackle-quockle-quackle".' She laughed quietly as she imitated the ghost's chatter. Then she said: 'He lived with me for almost a year. It was so much fun with him. So lovely. My Quockle really loved singing. And he was always getting

up to mischief. Once, we were in the attic, right above my flat here. There's that little window with the bars on that reaches down to the floor, do you know the one? We sat high above the town and threw porridge oats down on everyone who walked past. It was the middle of summer, I was barefoot, and every time Quockle let the oats trickle down, he cried out: "It's snowing! It's snowing!"' Mrs Wilhelm's shoulders shook as she laughed soundlessly.

Paul looked at the frail old Mrs Wilhelm who had apparently once sat barefoot up in the attic, dangling her little legs in the air and laughing as she threw porridge oats down into the street.

'And Quockle loved coal,' said Mrs Wilhelm.

'Coal?' asked Paul.

'There was no central heating then,' explained Mrs Wilhelm. 'We had a stove in the kitchen and a fireplace in the sitting room. They were both heated with coal briquettes, sort of black lumps of coal. Quockle used to rub himself on them until he was all covered in coal dust, and he loved it because he thought it made him look scarier.'

'And how did you lose Quockle?' asked Paul.

'He was discovered one day. By a neighbour. While I was at school. It was probably his singing that gave him away. At any rate, a neighbour heard a voice in our flat and called the police because he thought it was burglars. The police broke down our door and took Quockle away. When I came home, the flat was wrecked. It must have been a pretty long chase. There were black marks on the walls; I think he must have just rubbed himself with coal dust and that was why he couldn't hide on the ceiling. The police took him to a top secret research institute and I never saw him again.' Mrs Wilhelm shook her head sadly.

'But . . .' said Paul. 'If it was such a top secret institute, how do you know about it?'

'I went to the police the next day and asked about Quockle. Two of the police officers just looked sternly at me and said there were no such things as ghosts and I should go home and never talk such rubbish again. But the third one was nice. He ran after me as I left in tears and told me about the institute. I even tried to break in to the place, but of course a security guard caught me and took me home. After that, I always hoped that Quockle would come back. Or another of his kind.'

Mrs Wilhelm fell silent and stared at her collection of locks for a long time. In the kitchen, you could hear the tap dripping to itself, but otherwise there wasn't a sound.

'Zippel,' said Paul.

'Sorry?' said Mrs Wilhelm.

'Mine's called Zippel.'

Mrs Wilhelm clapped her hands and threw back her head: 'Ziiippel!' she cried in delight. 'Wonderful! Tell me, does he say "Zippeldesticks" whenever he's annoyed?'

'Yes,' said Paul.

'Zippeldesticks,' repeated Mrs Wilhelm. 'Just like Quockle used to say.'

'Really?' mused Paul. 'Are they related?'

'I don't know,' said Mrs Wilhelm. 'But I do know one thing: they're quite right to be afraid of grown-ups.'

'Grow-nups,' said Paul, just the way Zippel always said it.

Mrs Wilhelm chuckled: 'Grow-nups, exactly.' Then she grew serious again: 'My parents glued up all the locks after that. They were very shocked that I had had a secret friend living with us for a year. And they were determined to stop any more keyhole ghosts joining us. I tried to explain to

them that Quockle was my best friend. They just nodded and said yes-yes, and then they still glued up all the locks.'

'So is it really true that keyhole ghosts always live in front doors?'

'Of course it's true.'

'Is that why you collect locks?'

'Yes. All my life, I hoped that another keyhole ghost would make his home with me. But instead one came to you. It's better that way. Your Zippel would just be bored with an old biddy like me. That's why . . .' She leaned on the arm of her chair, stood up slowly and walked over to the bookcase. 'That's why I'm giving you one of my locks. If I've understood correctly, your Zippel is in urgent need of a new home.' She looked at her collection. Then she pointed to an ornate, rectangular metal lock and said: 'He seems to have particularly liked this one. He must have been doing loop-the-loops in there, given how much dust whirled out of it.'

Paul saw that there was a little heap of rust and dust in front of the lock.

'Oh,' he said. 'Is that how you guessed that I've got a ghost too?'

'Well, it really wasn't very hard,' said Mrs Wilhelm, carefully lifting the large, angular lock down from the shelf. 'First, you were sitting here, staring at my bookcase. After you left, there were little piles of dust by all the locks. Then Mr Nitzsche hurt his eye. And shortly after that, there was that letter to Mr Nitzsche downstairs. When I asked Mr Nitzsche about it, he told me the strange thing that had happened to his flat. All in all, I didn't exactly need to be a great detective.'

She looked at Paul and said: 'I'm a hundred per cent on your side. But be more careful in future, do you hear? Both of you. I want Zippel to stay with you for ever.'

Paul nodded.

Mrs Wilhelm held the lock in both hands and passed it to Paul.

'Oh,' said Paul. 'It's pretty heavy.'

'Yes,' said Mrs Wilhelm. 'But very homelike, I think.'

'Thanks a lot,' said Paul. 'Really truly.'

'Please,' said Mrs Wilhelm, 'say hello to Zippel for me. You two can come up here any time.' She pointed to her lock collection. 'I'd be really very pleased if he used my playground now and again. And I'd like to tell him about

Quockle. It would be good for him to know that there are a few of his kind. But you should probably go now, or your parents will be wondering what's going on. Besides, I'm tired. But would you like to come back tomorrow?'

'Yes, please,' said Paul. 'Bye, Mrs Wilhelm.'

'Bye, Paul.'

Now, when she smiled at him, Paul found her face beautiful. All the lines around her damaged left eye looked like the wrinkles on a round, shrunken apple.

(HAPTER EiGHTEEN

That's almost the whole story. When Paul got back to his flat, there was a note on the kitchen table:

Dear Paul,
We've gone to the café for an ice cream to celebrate
Dad's new job.
Come and join us if you like.
Love,
Mum and Dad

But Paul wanted to celebrate something else entirely. He called out to Zippel, who had been hiding in his bedroom and now came floating out into the hall. When he saw the lock, he did such wild loop-the-loops down the whole

corridor that Paul was afraid he'd crash into a wall.

Then, together, they placed the lock in Paul's bookcase.

Zippel has slept there ever since. Every morning he says that he's never slept so well in all his life as in Mrs Wilhelm's lock, really truly. And that Mrs Wilhelm is the nicest grow-nup there is in the whole wide world.

When Mr Nitzsche came on Monday to change the lock, Paul even helped him, and not a single tool fell down the stairs, and no dust clouds came out of the lock either. But afterwards, all the tools in his toolbox were sorted by colour, and Zippel said that Mr Nitzsche is actually quite nice for a grow-nup too. And on Tuesday, Paul's mum had her opera performance, and she sang really beautifully. And Dad did more of the cooking after that, so there was less burnt pasta.

But on the evening that Paul's parents went out for ice cream, Zippel had to start settling in to his new home, and dust and rust flew all over the place while he sang a little keyhole-ghost-moving-in song. Once he had finally finished, Paul said that he wanted to try something out. And Zippel said that trying things out was always very good and what were they going to try out, then?

'Come on,' said Paul. And they went out onto the stairs, and right up to the sixth floor. And Zippel thought that they were visiting Mrs Wilhelm because he now liked her even better than he'd done before – *that Mrs Wilhelm, wow, super-duper, really truly.* But instead Paul climbed the narrow stairs up to the attic, where he'd never dared go alone before because it was all dark and empty and dusty up there. But with Zippel alongside him he didn't mind, and Zippel felt right at home in the dark and dust anyway. Paul saw that Mrs Wilhelm had been right – at the end of the attic there really was an ancient, barred window that reached down to the floor. When Paul opened the window, it creaked so horribly that Zippel said, 'Wow, that's a really good window.' Outside, the golden September sun was gilding all the rooftops and you could see the whole town, and Paul sat on the floor and dangled his legs through the iron bars, and Zippel sat very smartly beside him. He looked cautiously down the seven floors and said: 'Hoo-oo-oo, even for me that's very high.'

Paul pulled a bag that he'd brought from the kitchen out of his pocket, flung a pinch of flour into the air and said to Zippel: 'Look, snow in summer.'

Of course, Zippel loved it. Paul held the open bag out to him, Zippel dived into it, head first, flailed around wildly with his arms and cried: 'Warning, snowstorm! Warning, snowstorm!'

And so first there was a very quiet shower of flour-snow, and then a brief Zippelish flourstorm. Paul held onto the bag that was raising dust like a volcano, and looked out over the golden rooftops and he knew, he knew for absolute certain, that life with Zippel was going to be exciting and bold and beautiful. And in the distance, he could see the first cranes, which were already setting up the ghost train for Oktoberfest.

THE TRAIN MOUSE

Uwe Timm
Illustrated by Axel Scheffler

When Nibbles, an inquisitive young mouse, scampers onto a train
at the local station, little does he know he is about to be swept
away on a cross-country adventure. Nibbles travels to Switzerland
and France and finally ends up as the star performer in a circus
in England! But then Nibbles begins to feel homesick.
How will one little mouse find his way back again?

'Thoroughly charming' *LoveReading*